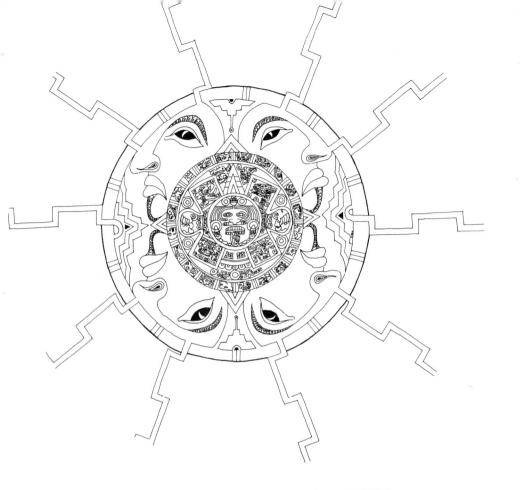

BLUE DAY ON MAIN STREET

BY

J. L. NAVARRO

A QUINTO SOL BOOK
1973

QUINTO SOL PUBLICATIONS, INC.
Publishers of Chicano Literature
P.O. BOX 9275
Berkeley, California 94709

First Printing: October 1973

Library of Congress Catalogue Card Number: 73-88742
ISBN NUMBER: 8-88412-063-5

BLUE

DAY

ON

MAIN

STREET

Art for *Blue Day on Main Street* by Edel Villagómez

THE COMMISSION

The area around Gig's Cafe on the Strip was shadowed with the shade of the afternoon. It was the end of March, the beginning of spring. The day was pleasantly warm with a mild, rambling breeze brushing against the incongruous variety of people that made up the Sunset Strip on any given day of the week.

Tony sat alone at one of the cafe tables, serene in posture and inwardly content to be alive on this fine spring day among the rest of the cafe's patrons. He was smoking a cigarette and drinking coffee as he watched the people pass by on the walk, looking more than once when an attractive girl came by, each time suppressing the urge to reach out and grab onto some cheek flesh. This would not have been altogether impossible, for the cafe was an imitation of a Paris sidewalk cafe where people lounge in the open air, grazing elbows with the passers-by.

At the moment he was casting a wishful gaze at a blonde hippie girl across the street. She was standing on the corner with a dozen or so copies of the Free Press tucked under her arm, looking expectantly at the traffic that was coming her way.

He noted, while bringing the coffee cup to his lips, that the hippie girl had enormously large breasts. Abnormally large, he thought, for a girl her age. In his estimation, she could not have been more than sixteen.

Tony sipped on his coffee, wondering how big the blonde's nipples were. Were they pink or brownish? Were they smooth or pimply? He casually drank in the image of her sybaritic body. Her buttocks and thighs seemed to want to burst from her bell-bottom capris.

Putting the coffee cup down, Tony began to wish he had brought his glasses along to see the girl's features more clearly. But he could not afford to wear his prescription glasses at this time. Not when he was working.

He sat reposed on the thin wire-structured chair, relaxed and self-confident behind his non-prescribed shades, one leg resting on the knee of the other, projecting the debonair style of the man-about-town. He plucked a bit of gray lint off his black tapered slacks; and then (unconsciously) he glanced over his heavy-knit olive green sweater, making sure there were no traces of last night's hamburger on the sleeves or chest area. This quick inspection was prompted by having observed a woman at the next table who had forked some tuna salad to her mouth only to have it fall from the prongs to her blouse. Her face turned crimson, her body rigid, and she forced an embarrassed grin on her escort.

Tony pretended not to have noticed and turned to look at the blonde across the street.

The insistent reverie . . . under the purple sheets . . . soft jazz . . . bottle of sherry . . . . Two glasses . . . and the blonde, nude . . . .

. . . *why?* . . .

Rebecca, why did you have to go to Italy?

Big tits . . . the blonde, nude . . . god, she has big tits.

. . . *for the culture* . . .

No time for pleasure.

His last commission had come to an abrupt end when Rebecca had gone to Italy with her husband. On a business trip. She was sorry, but Tony, of course, could not come along. It would be an indiscretion of which she would never hear the end; so she said, whatever that meant. Although, she had made him a present of a check guaranteed to carry him through for at least three months. It should be enough, she said, until you get yourself another. And, for consolation, she assured him that if nothing turned up before her return, she would be more than willing to have him back.

Now, two months later, sitting at the corner at Gig's Cafe on the Strip, almost penniless, Tony sat waiting for the next one. The one still unknown to him. He stared at the blonde, thinking, wondering who it would be. She would be old. They were always old. Not prunes, no. But old, matured women who invariably thought of themselves as sophisticated. He really didn't want another one. He wanted the blonde.

. . . the blonde. She was all smiles now. A car had pulled up and she sold a copy of the Free Press to the fat, bald man behind the wheel. The fat man didn't seem to be the Freep type reader. The ads, maybe?

What time, what day was it?

The money was running low and, to boot, Rebecca had wired him a message informing him that she would not be returning to the States with her husband as intended. She would be staying on in Naples to absorb more of the Italian culture. Wish you were here. . . .

It had come as no surprise to him. Women like Rebecca were the sole support of men like Tony, and they were just as (if not more) unpredictable and fickle as the men she dealt with. All the same, he thought. They're all the same. Only for the culture. Touring the sights, saving the important ones for later. In the end, all the same.

He looked across the street at the young blonde and wondered if perhaps he was getting old. He was only twenty-eight, and yet he felt ancient.

He shifted his eyes from the blonde to the women that passed on the walk and the women who sat around him in the cafe area. He caught the eye of quite a few of them. But they were either with escorts, or the look they gave him wasn't the look he was waiting for. And he knew the "look" well enough to distinguish a good prospect from a bad one. A bad prospect was a waste of time, and right now time was something he could not afford to waste. Of course, if circumstances began to lead down hill, he had dabbled with the idea of becoming a hippie. This mode of living was one he would not altogether go along with. But, if things got any worse, he would have no choice. Then again, the alternative didn't really seem a bad one, not while he watched the blonde hippie girl across the street.

On the sly, he cast a furtive glance at himself in the reflection of the cafe's window. The green pull-over sweater and black slacks looked well on him. His dark hair was not short, not long, combed back with a natural wave to it. He received an immediate impulse to smile at himself, but this would have been too immodest. As it was, while looking at himself, he was making as if he were searching for someone inside the cafe. On the other side of the pane, beyond his reflection, he saw a waiter zig zagging through the tables with a tray of food and drinks. In the reflection of the street he could see the blonde hippie girl standing on the corner.

Then, as if she had suddenly materialized, he noticed that a tall woman was standing next to him, or rather behind him. When he turned to look up at her, she smiled at him and said, "May I sit down?"

A pang of joy swept over him as he watched the evenness of the woman's false teeth. Her smile was captivating.

"It's such a lovely day," she said. "I am a bit tired. And the other tables all seem to be crowded."

"It's perfectly all right. I was getting lonely sitting here by myself anyway."

"That makes two of us," the woman said, pulling the chair out to sit down. "My name's Helen."

"My name's Tony."

"I'm very pleased to meet you, Tony."

He looked at the woman, trying to appraise her status. She was a pleasant enough looking woman, pretty and youthful, who wore the appropriate modern-conservative apparel of the day. Somehow she represented a retired actress, not retired by age, but rather by lack of parts—or talent. Whatever, she seemed fashionable enough to him to further pursue their relationship. After all, a job was a job.

"Would you like anything?" he asked.

"No, really, it's quite all right. I have—"

"I insist," he said.

She spread the luster of her gray eyes on him as if observing a poor but gallant young man.

Maybe she was wise. Somehow he knew that this wasn't her second time around.

"What will it be?" he said.

"Oh, a glass of lemonade will be fine."

"You know," said Helen. "You remind me a lot of my son. He was killed in the war."

Tony had an itch to ask which war it had been, but decided against it. Best to be prudent.

The woman though, anticipating the question, answered, "In the Korean War."

The waitress came back and set the glass of lemonade and cup of coffee down on the table. Tony watched her huge behind tumble in rhythm as she walked away.

"A very lovely girl," said Helen. "She gave you a rather friendly smile. Do you know her?"

"She's a friend of mine." He smiled at the woman. *But no money.*

"My son . . ." Helen lapsed her words with a sigh and lifted her head to the high clouds, not with a searching gaze but with a certainty in her eyes. "Oh, he was popular, too—with the girls. He was such a well liked, friendly young man. Handsome, outgoing." She looked at Tony, inquiring his face and seeing herself in the reflection of his shades. "He would have been thirty by now. I hope you don't mind me asking, but . . . how old are you?"

Before Tony could catch himself, the lie had slipped out:

"Twenty-four."

"Really?" said Helen with surprise. "My, you certainly are mature looking for your age."

The annoyance this caused Tony was quickly covered up with as gracious a response as he could manage.

"Thank you."

He smiled at her, exposing his front clip-ons, and drank some coffee. Through the corner of his eye, he glanced at the young hippie girl across the street.

God, she has big tits.

. . . wish you were here . . .

"My son was a student of engineering at Yale before he enlisted. He didn't have to go, you know. Oh no. He could easily have been deferred. A top student all the way." Again, she looked up at the sky, focusing her eyes on the pinnacle of a cloud strung at midnoon. "I suppose it was his sense of duty that prompted him to act so rash," she said, as if speaking to the cloud she watched. "He was such a brilliant young man." She turned hastily to Tony. "Excuse me if I seem overly boastful about Wendell. But I was so very proud of him."

Tony, keeping pace, just smiled.

"I remember the time Wendell and Sue Ann went out together. I remember it as if it were yesterday. It was their first date. For the both of them. Oh, my, you should have seen the look on Wendell's face when he came . . ."

Tony tuned all his attention to Helen's face. Classic features, delicate, lovely. Her skin, creamy white, for a woman her age was excitingly smooth, soft looking. The only lines on her face were thin lines that parenthesized her mouth, and they were only acutely noticed when she smiled. Her chestnut hair was pinned up, stacked high on her head, and she had a beauty mole between her neck and collar bone. Tony visualized her in the nude. He imagined her body to be firm, fleshy and well preserved; her arms, the curve of her legs, the rounding quality of cleavage of her breasts, all gave indications that she was a woman still well equipped with the essential necessities.

The breeze came in gently around them and with it the fragrance of the woman's body stirred in Tony's direction. Excellent, he thought. Exact. So many women her age wore scents that did not at all become them. They were either too sweet or too poignant. But this woman, Helen, was scented with a subdued aroma that suggested her style in sex: Dim room, not totally dark, easy movements, and when passion reaches its meridian, the heat goes up and . . .

"Did you go to college?" she asked.

"For a while. I didn't care too much for it."

"I'm surprised to hear that. You seem to be a bright young man. What do you do?"

"Nothing. That is, nothing academic."

Helen took a lady-like sip from her lemonade, and said, "What are you doing? I mean, what do you do now?"

"Like I said: Nothing. Actually I'm unemployed at the moment."

"Ohhhhh?" she said. "It seems to me that a young man with your fine appearance should have no difficulty in obtaining work."

"Well, frankly, I am looking for work."

"Anything in particular?"

"You might say so, yes."

"Wendell, my son, worked as a parking lot attendant for a while. He even worked in a car wash. God knows, he didn't have to. We—my husband and I—had no complaints about his choice of jobs. These were summer jobs, of course, when he was still in high school. I suppose he wanted to know what the lower-strata of boys were like. Wendell had a tremendously inquisitive mind and he was such a great humanitarian. You know, to this very day, I keep telling myself that he would have made an excellent Peace Corps worker."

Her husband? (Tony had pegged her for sure as a wealthy widow.) *Maybe I'm getting rusty.*

"Are your parents living here in Los Angeles?"

"No," he said. "They live in San Francisco."

In San Francisco. Never the same place twice. With Rebecca it had been New Orleans. Always a lie. The brief sketches he gave of his past were always slightly distorted, and by this very act of altering his past he achieved a feeling of physical and mental restoration.

"San Francisco," Helen said. "Oh, what a fine town. Wendell spent a summer there once with some friends of his. Some Japanese boys he met at a scout jamboree." She lifted her head to the sky. "Wendell had such a high feeling of self-esteem. He was a model boy all through his childhood, and as a teenager he participated only in the valued conformities of the community. Why, he made eagle scout in half the time it takes the average boy. Were you ever in the boy scouts?"

"No," said Tony. "I never cared too much for their uniforms."

"Ahhhhh," said Helen, as if it were indeed a shame. "It would have been a marvelous experience for you. Somehow I can't help thinking of you as a former boy scout. I don't know quite how to explain it. There's a certain look about you—"

Tony was beginning to think that the woman was just wasting his time. All this talk about her son was boring him. Maybe all she wanted was some one to talk to who might have been her son. One of those. The milk and cookie type. Although, her appearance didn't suggest this. She radiated too much sensuality. Her physical structure and her manner of comport did not at all agree with each other. But, of course, they came in all shapes and sizes, physically and mentally. In the past, though, he had never met a woman quite as nebulous as the woman he faced now.

"My husband was in the bologna business," Helen said. "Poor dear, he loved his work so much that it resulted in his end. Wendell and I were forever urging him to guard his health. But Henry was a proud man, and stubborn, too. He had ulcers, you know. A horrible fate, under the circumstances. He was something of a fanatic, I suppose, when it came to his work. Doctor Lank had put him on a strict diet for his weight and ulcers. Only Henry would not leave his product alone. For eighteen years he packed bologna sandwiches for work, and he devoured them with apparent relish in front of his employees five days out of the week, never once letting them know the unfortunate condition of his stomach. Yes, Henry was a proud man. Wendell respected him highly. He would still have been around today if it hadn't been for his pride. He was fond of saying, I remember quite clearly, 'If my bologna is good enough for the people, then it's certainly good enough for me.' He was a bit of a leftist when it came to his business."

I knew it, Tony thought. He felt a great deal of reassurance in what Helen had said. His sense of prey was still intact.

But what about the commission? As in a chess game, it was easy to foresee one or two moves ahead, possibly three. Only the outcome was always a dubious haze. And, now, he certainly wasn't going to settle for a stalemate.

"The bologna wasn't what killed him though," said Helen. "Although, indirectly, I suppose it did. . . ."

Bologna factory? The bologna business must bring in good money. Only for the commodities of living well. Gadgets were always an attraction.

". . . he died that way, poor dear. Wendell had begged him, implored him to stay home. His ulcers were acting up, you know. But Henry would not heed—"

Didn't she say he died? In the factory?

"The factory?" he said, inching his ear to her with interest. "What happened?"

"Well, like I said, a crate of bologna fell on his head. He was taking his p.r. man and photographer on a tour of the company. Wendell begged him not to go. But no. With two bologna sandwiches in his briefcase, Henry went off to the plant. While he was pointing out a new processing machine to his p.r. man, down comes this crate of bologna from a pile of others onto Henry's head. It seems ironic that Henry suffered and was killed by the very bologna that he cherished above everything else in the world. First the ulcers, and then the crate that split his head like a knife cleaving a log of bologna."

How poetic . . . a log of bologna.

"Oh, I shudder to think of it," she said. "What a deploring topic. Everytime I recall the tragedy I—" She sniffled and from her purse she brought out a thin, slightly scented handkerchief. She dabbed at her nostrils and then she broke her mood into a concise laugh. "How foolish of me. You must think I'm a sentimental old hen."

"Of course not. You must have loved him very much."

The blonde, for the first time, was looking in Tony's direction.

"Oh, I did, I did. He wasn't an attractive man, by any standards. But, oh, I don't know. . . . I sometimes—"

. . . want to know you better than the image of you. Touch your golden hair. You're an object at a distance. Space conquers over us. I quench only on your image. I will never hear a greeting, initial statement from you. Only your image. Your tits, thighs, long blonde hair . . . at a distance . . . only . . .

"... we were poles apart. I was much closer to Wendell, in all respects. We shared our troubles, our joys' and triumphs together. Everything. ... Henry was more of a dear friend to me than a husband, really, and far from being a lover." Helen snatched quick glances about her, moving her already parting lips to Tony. "Sexually he wasn't very active. The bologna business took up most of his energy. It seems a pity. To have lived for work alone. Wendell, on the other hand, loved work, but he took time out for pleasure as well. Simple, everyday pleasures that make life worth living. Why, if it hadn't been for Wendell I don't know what I would have done with myself. Sex, oh yes. My, was he sexy. Trim and muscled body. A model boy if there ever was one. Such dimensions!" A slow sigh expired as her head rose to the sky.

While Helen contemplated the clouds, Tony allowed himself a long desirous gaze at the blonde.

He turned to Helen.

Heads or tails, win or lose, time to lay it on the line.

"Are you doing anything tonight?"

Helen brought her eyes down from the sky with a puzzled look on her face. "Pardon?"

"Have you got any engagements this evening?"

"No. I don't believe I have." She watched him, transfixed, almost as if she were seeing some one else. "Why do you ask?"

"No special reason. I just thought we might spend the evening together."

"Why, it sounds lovely. Yes, I like that very much. Together, just the two of us." She looked at him for a long while. Then she said, "Do you mind?" and she reached out her hand to take his shades off. She looked into his eyes, searching for something he knew wasn't there. "Perhaps we better leave now. You know how long it takes a woman to get ready."

At her house, an elaborate layout in the Hollywood Hills, well secluded in the density of surrounding trees and bushes, they drank brandy while Helen changed into something more formal, and she chatted about Wendell and the many great times they had together.

From her bedroom, she called, "Make yourself at home. Feel free to look around if you wish."

Tony, who had been sitting on the living room couch, stood with brandy-on-the-rocks in hand and began to amble about the house.

He toured the kitchen, the backyard, the den, a guest room, and the library before he came to the room with the blue door. He opened the door and felt for the light switch along the wall. The room had no window. The switch was of the variety that one pushes in and has touch control over the intensity of light desired. The light was blue in its globe incasement. He turned the circular control to the highest degree of light.

The room, surprisingly, was modestly furnished in comparison to the rest of the house. It curiously resembled a motel room. There was only a bed and two chairs, a bureau, and a nightstand. On the floor, Tony felt the soft cushiony red rug beneath his feet. The room itself was not very large, and the object that commanded immediate attention was the single bed with its resplendent purple spread. The second most striking thing about the room was its walls. There were no paintings on them; rather, they were decorated with many 8x11 photographs of males. All young. Most of the pictures were full-face shots.

Tony was carefully examining the photo of a young man whom he thought he recognized when Helen suddenly came into the room.

"Ah, here you are. I was beginning to wonder where you had disappeared to. I see you found your way to Wendell's room."

Of course, he thought. It could be no one else's room but his.

"Who are all these men?"

"Wendell's friends. He had many friends, as you can see. He was a very popular boy, Wendell."

Yes, Tony thought; and apparently partial to displaying only his male companions. There was not a single female's picture on any of the four walls.

"We had better be going," Helen said, heading for the door.

Before leaving, Tony went to the picture of the young man whom he thought he knew and read the scripture: To Mother with Love, Wendell.

"Hurry," Helen called, "or we'll never be out of here."

. . . with Love, Wendell . . .

Tony knew he recognized the face from somewhere, and he was sure that it was not Wendell.

They went to a Chinese restaurant on Santa Monica Boulevard. Helen had suggested going there. Wendell had taken her there often, she said.

After dinner, Tony suggested an underground movie.

"Certainly," said Helen; hardly letting a minute go by without adding, "I don't know when I've had more fun. Wendell and I used to do this often."

It was past two when they arrived back at her house. Tony hadn't even hinted at going there. While she drove home she acted as if Tony had all the right in the world to be with her.

When they stepped into the living room, Helen said, "You may use Wendell's room tonight."

She led the way to the room with the air of an indifferent house maid. Tony opened the door and stepped in, expecting Helen to follow.

But no. Instead, she closed the door and Tony heard her muffled footsteps over the carpet, heading for her own quarters.

Is that all? The End? Over?

He suddenly felt like a character in a Disney flick. Like a hollow tin can.

There he stood, in the center of the small room, turning around in one spot, looking at the pictures on the walls. The pale blue light gave the faces eery contours, unearthly, the look of perverts. All evening Tony had wondered about the pictures, especially of the fellow whom he thought he knew. He went up to the photograph and studied it; then, the light being insufficient to kindle any significant clues, he struck a match. He examined the wild pep pill eyes, the smiling elastic mouth, and the huge dominating teeth recessed behind the thick lips. The face seemed to be all eyes and all teeth. Where had he seen that face before? The flame fed on the sliver of cardboard and neared uncomfortably to his fingertips. He blew it out, let it fall to the carpet and then crushed it in with his shoe. He lit another match, straining his mind to remember the face. He stared at the mouth, the teeth, the thick lips, the eyes, thought, but nothing came to mind.

Blowing the match out, he took one of the chairs and put it next to the bed. Sleep was weighing on his eyes. He began to take his clothes off, hanging each garment neatly over the back of the chair, stripping to the skin. Then he stood there naked, feeling like an object of observation by the gallery of inanimate eyes that stared at him from the walls.

He folded the blankets back and slipped himself between the clean, cool sheets. He turned on his side and faced the nightstand. The top of the stand was notched with numerous cigarette burns. Out of curiosity he opened the drawer of the stand and discovered a handsomely bound edition of the Marquis De Sade. It figures, he thought.

He closed the drawer, turned once again and shut his eyes, still seeing the blue light overhead, pale in his mind.

Slade? . . . Of course!

Tony threw the covers off and went to the picture of the male with the wild eyes and gargantuan teeth.

Herbert Slade. Herby the Hug Slade. New York '64. Of course. It was all so clear now. They had both been at a party that night. Tony had taken an interest in him because Slade was going around the room, hugging male and female alike. When he had come up to Tony his hug had been refused. Come on, come on, everyone said. He's Herby the Hug. Let him do his thing. Slade had been trying to pass himself off as a painter at the time.

What the hell, thought Tony. He looked at the scripture again: *To Mother with Love, Wendell.* Then he went from one picture to the next, examining the signatures. They all had the same dedication and signed by the same name. They only differed in handwriting.

Tony thought he began to understand what was going on. But it was too much to think of at the moment.

He went back to bed and sleep began to run through him like a pleasant drug. The back of his eyelids became screens on which he saw himself running through cornfields. Row after row of corn stalks and long yellow fibers protruding from the husks. . . . *Nude, voluptuous body running through the furrowed fields, laughing in the sun. The blond, running, wanting to be caught . . .*

. . . what are you doing in Naples? . . .

The door swung slowly into the room, rousing Tony out of his dream. He saw Helen's body silhouetted by the dim lights of the hallway. She wore nothing more than thin, tight black panties. Her breasts hung firm and round, nipples tense.

She stepped into the room, her hair now combed down in a flip like a young girl's.

"Wendell?" she whispered.

She came nearer the bed, taking small, dainty steps.

Tony watched her, saying nothing. He watched her until she came so close that he could smell the perfume on her body.

"Wendell? . . . Wendell, dear, are you awake? Mother's come to keep you company."

ON THE WAY TO FRISCO

He sat to the side of the road with a cardboard sign in his hand: San Francisco. The cars on the highway went by indifferently. The sun had now baked his skin a deep brown. His nose had begun to peel and the skin on his lips had become dry and cracked.

Robert Duarte waited for his next ride in the heat of the passing afternoon. He knew there would be another car. It was just a matter of time. The last ride had been a rancher in a half-ton. He had gone only this far. It hadn't been a bad ride from Los Angeles. He was now in Bakersfield.

Down the highway a car was approaching. With both hands he lifted the sign over his head. The car didn't appear as if it was going to slow down. But as it went by the brakes squealed and the car swerved over, off the highway onto the dirt shoulder of the road. Robert quickly picked up his small carpetbag and sign and ran over to the car. A girl with a turquoise Indian band around her head was driving. There was no one else with her.

"Get in," she said.

He opened the door and hopped in. The girl was good looking, with long straight brown hair. The car started off again.

"Going to Frisco, eh?"

"Yeah."

"You go to college there?"

"No. I'm going up to visit my brother."

"It's a nice town."

Robert agreed, though he didn't know first hand. He hadn't been there before.

"Are you a student?" he asked.

"No. I gave that up a long time ago."

She wore jeans and a country type, red and white checkered blouse, no make up. She needed none. Her complexion was smooth and tanned and her eyes were deep pools of blue with an endless depth to them.

"I'm going as far as Fresno," she said.

"That's okay," he said. "Do you live there?"

"No. Just visiting the area."

"Where abouts you from?"

"Out of state."

Robert wanted to ask where from out of state, but he refrained. There was a way about the girl that puzzled him. It was the mystery one finds in others when meeting them for the first time in an unknown land. She carried herself well, with the confidence of the truly independent person.

"My name's Robert," he said.

"Glad to meet you."

He waited for her to give her name. The girl said nothing. Then, she reached between the cleft of her breasts for a thin cigarette.

"Here," she said. "Get your head tight."

Robert reached for the joint and lit it. He took a few drags and passed it to the girl.

Letting out a cloud of smoke, he said, "Nice weather up here."

The girl nodded. "It's okay," she said, holding in her breath.

They didn't say anything more after this. They listened to the radio and passed the joint back and forth until it was reduced to cocktail length. Robert took a cigarette from his pocket and rolled the tip of it between his fingers, letting half an inch of tobacco drift out the window. He then slipped the roach in the space and tightened up the tip. Then he lit it.

Evening had begun to arrive by the time they got to Delano.

The girl said, "Listen, when we get to Fresno it's going to be dark. If you want you can stay with me tonight. You can start up early tomorrow."

"Thanks," he said. "If it's not too much trouble."

"No trouble. There's plenty of room."

When they came to Fresno the car bypassed the city until they were on roads that took them near grape fields and orange groves. It was now dark over the countryside. Finally they came to a lonely road, leaving the grape fields and orange groves behind. On either side of the road there were rolling fields. The car continued down the dark road, penetrating the night with its headlights.

At last, pulling the car to the side and parking, the girl said, "Here we are."

Looking out the windows, Robert saw a deserted land. There were no houses to be seen anywhere near where they were parked, nor had he seen any houses on the way here.

"Where are we?"

"This is where I'm staying."

Without arguing, he got out of the car and followed behind the girl. She went off to the side into a field over a path of beaten down grass. Robert looked ahead to see if he could see any lights from a house. He saw none. The field over which they walked was bumpy. The darkness outlined the foothills that surrounded them. Robert walked on, following the girl with his carpetbag in hand.

"Be careful," she warned. "There's a steep slope ahead."

They inched their way carefully down the slope of loose rocks. At the bottom of the slope there was a wide clearing, and up ahead Robert could see what looked like the sheen of water. It looked like a lake. Still he could not see any house nearby. They continued walking a bit and then, suddenly, the girl gave a soft whistle. It seemed to be a practiced whistle. A signal of some kind.

When they were near the edge of water, he saw a fire burning in the distance. The orange flame burned through the dense entanglement of branches and leaves. From the same direction of the fire site a similar whistle was heard. The girl responded with another whistle. Then some crackling of dry leaves was distinctly heard as if someone were approaching.

"That you, Miranda?"

"Yeah," the girl answered.

"Did you get it?"

"I got it."

Robert saw a stalking figure coming their way. When the figure approached them, a medium sized boy with long black hair stood before them. His hair was tied back with an Indian band not unlike the one the girl wore.

"How's Molasses?" she asked. "Is he feeling better?"

"He's okay. He's been waiting. How many did you get?"

"Twenty."

"That's good."

The boy now turned his attention to Robert.

"Who's that?"

"A friend of mine. He'll be spending the night with us. Robert, this is Chico. My cousin."

Chico extended his hand. "Hey, glad to meet you." Then, to Miranda, he said, "Let's go. Molasses' been waiting."

The two walked ahead. Miranda turned and said, "Come on, Robert. There's nothing to worry about."

He followed them to the campsite. There was a small tent to the side of the fire. It was a "pup" tent and the front flaps were pulled over so one couldn't see what was inside.

Chico went up to the tent. He said, "Molasses, Miranda's back."

Shortly, an old man came out. He was as big as a grizzly with a mane of white hair on his head and a long fluffy beard that spread on his face like a bush covered with snow.

Miranda said, "How do you feel, Molasses?"

The old man yawned. "Better," he said. "A little cold isn't going to keep an old buffalo like me down for long."

Molasses sneezed and looked at Robert inquiringly. He squinted his eyes and roved them over Robert.

"This is a friend of mine," said Miranda. "He's going to spend the night with us."

"Glad to have you, young man. If my granddaughter invited you then you're welcome to stay as long as you like." The old man turned back to the girl. "Did you get it, Miranda?"

"I sure did."

From her pocket Miranda took out a plastic bag filled with white capsules. She handed them to Molasses who took the bag with a large brown hand.

"Well," he said, "let's not waste any time." He took three capsules out and put them in his mouth. Then he went to a canteen that hung from the side of the tent and swallowed the capsules with water. He handed the bag to Chico who took two capsules out and downed them. Then he handed the bag to Miranda. She took one capsule out and washed it down with some water from the canteen.

"Want some?" she asked Robert.

"What is it?"

"Mescaline," she said. "It's good stuff."

Mescaline, he thought. It had been some time since he had gone up on mescaline.

"Sure," he said. He took a cap from the bag and downed it with water from the canteen.

After this Molasses took the sack and went inside to store them safely away. When he came back out Robert was sitting around the camp fire with Miranda and Chico. The old man came up to them and sat himself between his granddaughter and her cousin.

"Well," he said to Robert, "did you come up for the harvest?"

"No," he said. "I'm on my way up to Frisco."

"Nice town. Beautiful. The city is altogether a poem in concrete and design. I worked in the canneries there two years back."

For his size, the old man had an extremely gentle voice. He was like an eagle with the spirit of a tame canary.

"I've kicked around this world most of my life," he said. "And if there's anything I've found out about myself it's that I hate to be in one place too long. People like us have it in our blood to want the outdoors about us all the time. Miranda there is half Cherokee, I'm two thirds that. Chico, well he's been in the open country for as long as he can remember. Born and raised in Delano. Seems like when I'm in the city too long I start to feel like I'm dying. I can't explain what it is. It just happens."

Chico fed pieces of thin kindle wood to the crackling fire. The flames leaped in the center of the group with the joyful exigence of an excited dancer. Sounds from the river and the surrounding land were heard. Frogs croaked and crickets sang their songs and once in a while sounds of an animal scuttling across the fields of snarled trees and brush were heard.

Molasses sneezed, then he yawned, then he breathed in the fresh air around him. He seemed content. He said, "Peyote is the spiritual key to your soul. Mescaline, being the main alkaloid of the plant, is the next best thing to it. It tells you things you wouldn't otherwise know about yourself and of the things that surround you."

Robert, like the rest of them, waited for the mescaline to begin circling his mind. Molasses closed his eyes and a faint smile of pleasant expectation played on his bearded face. Robert looked at the three of them. He looked at Chico feeding the fire and he looked at Miranda sitting placidly and beautiful and at the old man who sat between them. Molasses was like a hermit king with his two subjects beside him.

"The freedom of a dog running free," he said. "The freedom of being independent. The freedom of a dog running free in the woods of a sylvan panorama. Seeking nothing and going nowhere."

"Molasses is a poet," said Miranda. "He has a whole box full of poems."

"I write poems for much the same reasons that others collect stamps," said Molasses. "Those who collect stamps attempt to collect a bit of the world. In writing poems I attempt to collect a bit of myself."

"What do you do, Robert?" Miranda asked.

"I go to U.C.L.A. I'm a social science major."

"Interesting work."

"It has its moments."

"Are you from L.A.?" asked Chico.

"Yeah."

"Lot of smog there."

"Too much smog."

"People should get back to the country," said Chico. "The simple ways of life."

"We've been on the road with Molasses now for over a year," said Miranda. "Ever since his wife died. I used to go to college up at Santa Cruz. I was going to be a teacher. At the time, Chico was working in a gas station."

"Lousy work to be doing for the rest of your life," Chico said. "I'm a drop-out."

"There's nothing like being on your own," said Molasses. "Nothing in the world."

"Last year after the orange harvest we went to Colorado and lived in a cave and we grew our own vegetables and hunted animals," said Miranda. "Chico's pretty good with the bow now. Before, he was using the .22 rifle to hunt. But Molasses told him he should use the bow instead."

"I'm almost as good as Molasses now," said Chico. "I can hit a moving target at twenty-five yards damn near every time."

"We might even go to Mexico after the harvest," said Miranda. "Molasses has some friends down there near Guadalajara."

"You're welcome to come with us if you like," said Chico.

"Thanks," said Robert. "But, well, I don't know."

"Think it over," said Miranda.

"You'll learn more about people on the road than in a classroom," said Molasses, "I'll tell you that."

Robert thought it over. Why should he go back to L.A.? Back to college? It was only to get that degree and then into a DPSS office to half-heartedly help the poor by giving them meager alms for their misery. Why not instead be a dog running free, traveling and living off the fat of the land? Yes, why not. What would he lose except something that was intangibly known as security. And why continue onto Frisco to visit his brother and his new bride? His brother that worked in the shipping department of some warehouse. He knew he would spend a month with them and then return to L.A., get a job and in the fall return for the new semester. He would do these things while the people he was with now went nowhere and to all places at once. To travel and to know other people and other places and to be free. To go to Mexico after the orange harvest, he thought, or to Colorado to live in a cave and to hunt with Chico and to sit around the camp fire at night and read Molasses' poems, to enjoy Miranda's beauty every day of the week and not just for one night. It was a beautiful life shared with beautiful people. But Robert knew that it would be impossible for him to share it with them. For the moment he was content to be with them. Even if only for one night.

Chico got up and went to the tent. He came back with a portable radio. It was a big radio with a short wave band. He switched it on. The music came to them instantly and filled the area with bluesy sounds:

   . . . bye bye, baby, bye bye
      too late to worry
     bye bye, baby, bye bye . . .

The fire leaped up and crackled and the embers burst in small volcanic explosions. The mescaline began running its soothing current over Robert's body in the manner in which only mescaline can do.

"Drugs render unusually good sensations," said Molasses.

"It's coming on," said Chico.

"Yes," said Molasses. "I can feel it. God bless mescal."

Chico brought rolled joints from his pocket. He passed them around. Molasses lit his and so did the rest. Robert looked at Miranda, sitting relaxed and with a smile as warm as the heat that warmed his hands from the fire. Her blue eyes flashed and flared in the light of the orange flames. He fell in love with her at that moment. He felt that he could love her for the rest of his life. The sky was star-studded and each star was winking at them. The constellations were on display for them, an art gallery in the sky magically showing the works of nature. They were silent. Listening to the night sounds around them, inhaling marijuana with the fresh air of the outdoors. Molasses smiled a smile that was followed by whimsical chuckles as he put his large hands over the fire. Robert knew he was being tickled by the mescaline. He felt a strong bond of affection for these roving gypsies and for the way they lived life.

Miranda stood up. She said, "Let's go for a walk, Robert."

Robert looked at Molasses and Chico.

"It's alright," Chico said.

"Go on," said Molasses.

He got up and they walked down river over a narrow trail that banked alongside of a steep hill. The brilliance of the colors about him were now intensified by the mescaline, bolder and more dense. The smell of the nearby orange groves was in the wind.

Miranda finally came to stop at a small clearing near the edge of the river. She sat down. The water of the river was a green sheet of glass. Robert turned to look at the campsite. He could see the fire and the dark silhouettes of Chico and Molasses.

"Sit down," Miranda said.

Robert sat down beside her.

"Look," she said. "A water snake."

On the surface of the river Robert saw what looked like a thin black rope zig-zagging over the water.

"There's a lot of water snakes around here," she said.

"Do you ever go swimming?"

"Sometimes. Mostly I go fishing though. There's lots of fish in the river."

"You people really live a free kind of life, don't you?"

"I suppose. It's as free a life as anyone can live. What surprises me is that more people don't live our kind of life. It's not really as hard as you might think. It takes getting used to, like anything else. But after a while you learn to do things you may have thought you couldn't do. Like fishing and hunting and making camp and growing your own vegetables. And not just once in a while, but all the time. Do you understand what I'm trying to say?"

"I think so."

"I guess there are people who couldn't do it though. Like those who have been softened by city life."

"I guess I'm one of those people," Robert said.

"I don't know. You're still young. You could get used to it."

"Maybe."

"I think you could. If you gave yourself half the chance."

"I think I'd be afraid to try."

"And I think I'd be afraid to go back to city life. There's more danger in living that kind of life."

"It's easier though."

"That's a matter of opinion."

Robert picked up some stones and tossed them in the river.

"I thought you said you were from out of state."

"I am," she said. "Why do you ask?"

"You said you were going to Santa Cruz."

"I did. But I'm originally from New Mexico. One day I decided to come to California to visit Chico and his parents. Then I started going to Santa Cruz. Then, when I was home on a weekend Molasses showed up and he got to talking about what he was going to do. Chico and I listened and we liked what we heard and here we are. I haven't regretted it once."

"What about the future?" he asked. "Don't you ever think of the future?"

"Not really. Only as far as tomorrow. That's what gives people ulcers. Thinking about the future. You never know what the future brings so there's no sense in thinking about it."

"I guess maybe you're right," he said.

"You know why?"

"Why what?" he said.

"About the future."

"What about the future?"

"One shouldn't think about it. Back at the camp I think I fell in love with you. I didn't count on it happening. It just did."

"It's funny that you should say that," he said. "I think I fell in love with you too."

"See," she said. "You never know what the future brings. Did you think you were going to fall in love with some one today, while you were out there waiting for a ride this afternoon?"

"No."

"That's what I mean. You never know about the future."

"I think that maybe we don't know what we're talking about."

"Why?"

"Love. I don't think we love each other."

"I do," she said. "I know how I feel. Right now I feel love. Tomorrow it might be gone."

Robert felt something for her also. Whether or not it was love he didn't know. But it was a pleasant feeling, not at all sensual desire. It was different. Unexplainable.

"It's a beautiful night," said Miranda.

Robert agreed.

"It's a beautiful night to make love," she said. "Right now the feeling I have for you is enough for me to want to share my body with you."

He turned to her. She was looking at him while she undid her blouse. There was no need to explain anything.

For the moment they loved each other. And for the moment that was all that mattered.

Gently and slow, their kisses and their embrace held them together for a long while. They didn't speak. The mescaline spoke for them, directing their movements like nature directs the waves of the sea.

That night they shared the same sleeping bag.

And the next morning, before Robert woke, Chico and Molasses had gone out to hunt rabbit. When Robert was up, the rabbits were roasting on a spit over a fresh fire. The four of them ate slowly and quietly while the morning came and with it a new sun and a new day. Today Robert would be on his way again.

After breakfast Robert said farewell to Molasses and Chico and then Miranda drove him back to the highway.

"Where should I drop you off?" she said.

"Anywhere around here will be fine."

She pulled the car to the side of the road.

"You sure you won't change your mind?" she asked.

"I can't. Some people can do what others just can't."

"I understand," she said. "So long, Robert."

He kissed her for the last time. "Good-by," he said.

The car drove off. Robert watched it disappear down the highway.

> . . . bye bye, baby, bye bye
> too late to worry
> bye bye, baby, bye bye . . .

He sat down and rested against a chain-link fence, placing the white cardboard sign before him. The sun was rising fast. It's going to be a warm day, he thought.

A RING FOR SONYA

Carlos Armenta walked down the cart path that led away from his village. The path sloped down to the wide Valley of El Pero. Below, off to the right, he could see the green water of the lagoon, and across from the lagoon there were the long, stretching fields of marijuana that Carlos worked with the others of his village and those of the surrounding villages. The marijuana was ready for harvest, he thought. Beyond the fields there were hills and beyond them the high mountains that appeared like jagged pieces of chocolate in the horizon. The evening sun was a bright orange ball, pinnacled on one of the lofty mountain ridges.

Carlos was on his way to Mota, the largest village in the region, five miles away. He made this trip from his village to Mota every day of the week, and he had been doing this ever since he had met Sonya Arias three months before. She was one of the girls who worked in María Solano's cantina, and she was by far the most beautiful. She was not in the stable of whores there. She was much too good for that. She was a dancer and a singer. And she chose her own men and made sure that it was not the other way around.

The people of his village knew how he felt about the girl in Mota. Some of the villagers said that he was wasting his time with a girl of Sonya's temperament. They said she was too wild for him. He should take a girl from the village to be his wife, a girl who would know how to treat him. His mother was the most unyielding adviser regarding his affections for Sonya. Doña Teresa, his mother, had fallen severely ill after discovering that her only son was pursuing a girl who worked in María Solano's cantina. "Those tramps are nothing but trouble makers," she would tell him. But Carlos listened to her about as much as he listened to the others. In the end he had become so weary of his mother's advice that he had moved out and built a shanty of his own on a vacant piece of land. He had not seen Doña Teresa now for some time.

A girl from the village was coming from the lagoon and heading in Carlos' direction. Her name was Andrea. She carried two water buckets, held by ropes attached to a beam of timber that was supported by her shoulders. Andrea walked sure-footed in her sandals as she came up the path. She carefully balanced the buckets as she walked.

Carlos approached her with some expectation. At one time the villagers had expected them to get married. There had been all indications of this in their relationship. They had seemed almost inseparable; until the night he left María Solano's cantina with Sonya. He had seen Sonya there before on other occasions. He had liked her. But he had never spoken to her until that night. Carlos had done a lot of drinking and he ended up talking to her for the first time since he had been going to the cantina. Later that evening he had taken her to the fields and there he made love to her. Thereafter he had not thought of any other girl but Sonya.

Andrea stopped just as Carlos was going to walk past.

"Don't you greet people anymore, Carlos?"

"Oh, good evening, Andrea. I'm sorry, but I'm in a hurry."

"Are you afraid that she might be gone when you get there?"

He ignored the question. He did not want to talk. He wanted to go his way without discussing what everyone thought was stupidity on his part. But he could not be unfriendly. "How's your family?" he said.

"Fine, thank you. I have news of your mother, Carlos."

"Is she better?"

"Yes. Doctor Orbo says she will be well soon. It would be a good idea if you went to visit her. She's begun to wonder what's happened to you."

"Tell her I'm fine and not to worry."

"You know how she feels about me."

"Not you. It's the girl in Mota."

"It's best if I stay away. The less we argue about Sonya the better it will be for her health."

"Perhaps you are right," said Andrea. "But maybe she is also right about her. She is not a village girl. She does not understand your ways, Carlos."

Carlos fingered the silver ring in his pocket. He had bought the ring from El señor Herrera, the local *brujo* that lived in a cave in one of the nearby hills. It had cost him many months of working in the fields. But it was not an ordinary ring. El señor Herrera assured him that it would render the love of whoever wore it to Carlos. That he was a peasant of the fields, and that Sonya was a girl who worked in María Solano's cantina, didn't bother him in the least.

"Love can bring together even the most uncommon people," he said.

"Does she love you?"

He felt the ring in his pocket. "Yes, Andrea. She loves me very much." And then, as if he had to prove this, he was compelled to bring out the ring and show it to her. "I even have this for her. She is going to be my wife."

"Has she already accepted?"

"Yes." It was a lie, but later this evening it would be true. He put the ring back in his pocket.

"I'm glad for her, Carlos. And for you too. I guess the rest of us were wrong about you and her."

"Well, thank you, Andrea, for the both of us. And you're invited to the wedding."

"When will it be?"

"Soon. Very soon."

"Should I tell your mother?"

"No. She will hear of it. I will tell her myself."

"Well, I better not keep the bride waiting," she said. "I'd better go."

"It was nice seeing you again, Andrea. Give my regards to your family."

He watched her walk up the path to the village. A group of naked children were playing and running around at the summit of the hill. The disappearing sun was throwing orange light on the shacks of the village.

Night had come when Carlos entered Mota. As he was crossing the street he could hear the usual commotion and goings on from the patrons in María Solano's cantina; the laughter and the drunken shrieks from the men and the high,shrilly voices of the women who kept the men happy and kept them coming back night after night for the pleasures that they relinquished to them for a few *pesetas*.

Carlos stepped into the cantina with a wide smile. There was thick and cloudy smoke everywhere. Smoke from tobacco and the sweet smelling smoke from marijuana. He scanned the people at the bar and at the tables and the ones who were dancing, to see if Sonya was among them.

"Ah!" said Jaime. "Look who's here. The sheep of the fields."

"How are you, Carlos?" greeted another. "You look well and happy."

"I am, my friend. I am. I bring good news for all of you."

"And what is it?" said a man with a clown's face. "Are you buying cervezas for me and my camaradas?"

"No," said Carlos. "I bring you news of my wedding. You are all invited."

"And who would be so foolish as to marry you, Carlos," said Jaime good naturedly. "You are still a boy, not yet a man."

"I am more of a man than you will ever be," said Carlos. "Where is Sonya? I have something for her."

"Sonya?" said María Solano who was behind the bar counter. "She is not here."

"Where is she?"

"I don't know," said María Solano.

"I hear that Armando Sencias is back for the harvest," said the man with the clown's face.

"Yes," said another. "And you know who his favorite woman is."

"Did Sonya go with him?" Carlos asked.

"What do you think, Carlos?" said Jaime.

"You better go home, Carlos," said María Solano. "There is nothing here for you."

"Sonya is going to be my wife," he said. "Look, I have this ring for her. I must know where she is."

The faces around the cantina stared at him without speaking. He knew that if Armando Sencias was back in the village that Sonya was with him. They did not have to tell him this.

"If you want," said a plump woman at the bar, "I will be your wife for the night."

The cantina went into an uproar of laughter.

"She will make you a good wife," said Jaime. "I have had her for my wife before."

Carlos turned to leave, saying as he went, "You are all invited to the wedding!"

The laughter from the cantina followed him as he went out.

There was a small hotel in Mota, the only hotel in the village. Carlos knew that Armando Sencias stayed in this hotel when he came to harvest the marijuana. But when he arrived there the proprietor told him that Armando had not checked in. The room that was always reserved for him was still vacant, he said. Carlos thanked the old man and left, worried now that perhaps Armando had taken Sonya away to marry her, although this did not seem likely. Armando was not the marrying kind. Still, the thought, the possibility of this being true, alarmed him.

He decided to visit Sr. Herrera. If anyone knew where they would be, it would be he.

He went out of Mota to the nearby hills. At the foot of one of the hills he began to scale the spiraling trail. As he climbed, the night wind howled through the darkness around him. When he reached the summit of the trail, Carlos could see the shadows inside the cave leaping like giant spirits on the pitted walls that were adorned with animal skulls and human skulls and other artifacts of the witch doctor's trade. He entered the cave and saw the *brujo* in his customary position, sitting cross-legged before a circle of fire. Each time Carlos came here the old man was in the same position. It was a rare thing to see him standing on his feet. He was like an ominous eagle perched on a patch of animal hide. The *brujo* Herrera, leather brown and streaked with wrinkles, sat motionless, staring at Carlos through slanted eyes that seemed not to see him.

"Sr. Herrera," he said, "I need your help."

The old man sat and stared and said nothing. He appeared not to be breathing, looking like a bronze figure with only his eyes emitting signs of life.

"Sonya is gone and I don't know where to find her," said Carlos. "You must help me."

"I can tell you nothing," said the old man.

"But I must find her to give her the ring."

Again, the *brujo* said, "I can tell you nothing."

The old man closed his eyes as if to say that the visit was over. He sat like a still corpse with his hands on his bony knees. The fire crackled and the tall shadows danced around the cave. Carlos did not understand why he would not speak to him. With a sense of disappointment he left the cave with the *brujo* sitting before the fire.

On his way home, Carlos took the long way by the river. He cut across the corn field that once belonged to Santiago Apodaca, the man who had slain his own family and afterwards hanged himself for no apparent reason. Some said that the *brujo* had put a curse on him.

Carlos was coming to Santiago's ranch house when he noticed that there were lights in the windows. Then he saw Armando Sencias' truck. The large red truck with the high panels that he used to haul the bricks of marijuana to the transporters that would take them to El Paso, T.J. and Yuma. "So this is where they are," he thought. His heart began to beat with excitement. He quickened his pace. When he came to the front porch he peered into one of the windows. Sonya was sitting at the table with Armando. She was talking and the man was drinking wine from a bottle. Carlos went to the door and knocked. He waited nervously, anxious to place the ring on Sonya's finger.

When the door was opened, Sonya stood on the other side.

Surprised, she said, "Carlos, what are you doing here?"

"I have come to talk to you, Sonya."

"I'm busy right now. Can't it wait?"

"No. I must talk to you now."

"Tomorrow, Carlos."

"I have something for you, Sonya."

"Yes? What is it?"

He produced the ring. The silver circle lay in his palm.

"This is for you. I want you to have it."

"How nice of you, Carlos. Thank you."

"Put it on, Sonya. Here." He took her left hand and slipped the ring on her finger.

"It's very lovely," she said.

Carlos waited for the charm of the ring to take effect.

"I must go now."

"Wait," he said. "Wait one moment."

"Carlos, I like the ring very much. And I like you. But right now I'm busy. I will see you tomorrow."

She pouted her lips and blew a kiss at him with her hand and then she shut the door.

HARVEST SEASON

The paths between the orange groves were now peopled with the migrant workers who, from early morning to dusk, labored to pick the trees free of the fruit they held. It was a hot season. The workers kept themselves going by singing songs and telling jokes and talking of past adventures in the fields. The men wore sweat bands around their heads, and the women wore bandanas over their heads. Some stood on ladders to get to the high oranges, those reputed to be the best because they caught more sun than those which were picked from the ground.

In one grove there were two people working by themselves. Standing midway on a ladder was Nancy and on the ground, catching the oranges she picked, was Timmy. At one time they had been man and wife. Divorced now, they had met at this camp unknowing that they would run into each other. They worked silently. It was only today that they had run into each other. Timmy had been in camp for over a week, since the season opened. Nancy had come in last night to sign on; and today they ran into each other. It had been a pleasant surprise for him, though he could tell that Nancy didn't feel the same. Moments before she had tossed words at him that were sharpened to dagger sharpness. He, quiet, just listened, hoping the exertion of her efforts to be rid of him would cool her off.

"Leave me alone," she had said. "Go work with the others."

He stood his ground, catching the oranges she tossed to him.

Now they were silent, working without saying a word. Just like the old days, he thought. They had been divorced for two years. The last time they had seen each other was in Oxnard during the strawberry season. And even then, when she found out that he was in camp, she had left the next day. That had been over a year and a half ago. Since then Timmy had traveled the migrant route hoping to run into her again, and this season in Fresno it had happened. He was sure that he still loved her. He had always been sure of this, even while she had filed for divorce. It had been a funny thing, the divorce. It had not been a funny thing at the time, but today thinking about it Timmy thought it amusing. It had all started over a girl by the name of Gloria. They had been in Indio harvesting dates at the time. One night Nancy had discovered him with her, under a date tree, in a most compromising position. Nancy, in a rage, pulled him off and there commenced an assault on Gloria while she lay nude and sweaty on the ground. He laughed to himself now, remembering the scene.

Nancy looked down from her ladder.

"What's so funny?" she said.

"I was just thinking of a joke Anselmo told me," he said.

Nancy turned back to her work. She picked the oranges and without turning let them fall to be caught by Timmy who in turn put them into crates. The warm breeze, carrying with it the scent of oranges, swept around them. He looked to the sky. The sun was past the meridian. He guessed the time to be somewhere between one-thirty and two. Before he could turn to catch the next falling orange, it came down suddenly on his head.

Rubbing his scalp, he said, "Watch what you're doing."

Nancy, looking down, said, "You watch what you're doing. I didn't tell you to help me. I can work this grove alone."

"You've always been able to do everything alone, haven't you?"

"I got along very well without you, if that's what you mean."

She went back to her work.

For the rest of the afternoon they said nothing to each other.

When quitting time rolled around they turned in their work sheets and were paid. Nancy was up ahead of him and when the foreman gave her her money she walked away as rapidly as she could. It took Timmy a running pace to catch up with her.

He called to her. "Hold on, Nancy."

She kept walking.

"Wait up, girl."

She didn't turn.

"Nancy!"

She didn't stop.

He quickened his step and when he caught up to her he caught her by the arm. Nancy rolled on her heels to face him with an anger he hadn't seen on her face since the night she caught him with Gloria. She wrested her arm free.

"Timmy, do me a favor. Get lost!"

"Can't we talk?"

"We have nothing to say."

She began walking again. Getting into step with her, he said, "I have a lot to talk about. Tell me what you've been doing with yourself."

"It's none of your business."

"I suppose it's not. Just curious. I haven't seen you for a long time. I've been wanting to."

"What's the matter? Traveling girls don't suit you anymore?"

"It's not that. Besides, you never know what you're going to get off them."

"That's what you deserve."

"Nancy, why can't we talk? Why do you have to be so far away?"

"Because I want it that way."

"You're being stubborn."

She stopped abruptly. Her tawny face was stern and resolute.

"Timmy, I don't care for you anymore. I'm going to get married next month to a real nice guy. We get along real fine. So please, leave me alone."

Timmy smiled. "Congratulations," he said. "Glad to hear it."

He meant what he said, though he also felt hurt. In the past he would torment himself by thinking of her. Wondering where she was, what she was doing, who she might be with. And today when they ran into each other again he felt the same elation he had felt the first time he had seen her before their marriage. And now, the discovery that she was getting married made him happy for her as well as sorry for himself, knowing he was at last going to lose her in marriage to someone else. In the past he never felt that he had lost her entirely. There was always that vague hope of seeing her again, of making her his again. Each time he went into a camp he had some expectation of her being there, or of her showing up unexpectedly. And behind his reveries, she remained his.

Cheerfully, he said, "Let's go somewhere for a drink. To celebrate."

"I'd rather not," she said, sounding, to some extent, friendly.

"Why not? I'm really glad to hear you're getting married. At least I'll have the satisfaction of knowing you'll be safe with someone. You know how camps are for women alone."

"Yeah," she said. "I've run into my share of trouble."

"Who's the lucky guy?"

"Someone I met in Monterey. He's a student."

"Getting classy, huh?"

"Not really. But I'm getting kind of tired of running the route."

It was a funny thing about Nancy and Timmy. Neither of them were born migrant workers. They did it because they both liked it. They both drifted into this life style. Whenever they told this to other workers they would look at them incredulously, unable to believe that anyone would do this sort of work of their own free will. But Timmy enjoyed the life of the migrant. He was originally from San Diego and Nancy from Los Angeles. They met in Arizona in the lettuce fields. Both had been on the road for a taste of something new. Timmy had just gotten out of the Army and Nancy had just pulled a semester at U.S.C. After the season they were married. A year and a half later they were beginning their divorce. And now here they were again, in the orange groves of Fresno.

"I thought you would have given this life up a long time ago," he said.

"So did I," she said. "Only when I find myself in a factory or in a packing plant and when the season is about to start I get this feeling like, well, I put my finger on the map and I'm on my way. After a while it gets in your blood. The traveling, the smell of the fields and the fresh air, the people."

"I feel the same way," he said. "Sometimes I tell myself I'm quitting to go to college or something. But I never do."

"Some people back home think I'm nuts for liking what I do, you know?"

"Yeah," he said. "I know."

They were walking now, toward the area where the workers parked their cars.

"Where are you staying?" he asked.

"In a singles cabin. And you?"

"Same."

It was evening now and the cool air from the north was coming on them in balmy gusts.

Timmy had grown to like the life of the vagabond attached to an area for only brief months and then on to another part of the country and other fields. Lately, he had been giving serious thought to joining the Peace Corps. It would fit his nature perfectly. Perhaps in South America. He knew the language. He was used to the hard life of the migrant. A life he welcomed like others welcome the leisure of an office position. And now he thought of going to South America through the Peace Corps, with Nancy. As man and wife. Again. Only she would be getting married soon. He would go though. Alone. After the season he would join and request South America as his locale.

"If you're getting married," he said, "why isn't your boy friend with you?"

"He'll be coming down in a week. I sent him a letter this morning telling him where I'm at."

"Are you going to make a campesino out of him?"

"For a season anyway. Then we'll be going back to college."

"You're going with him?"

"Yes."

"As a student or his wife?"

"Both."

"Well, good luck to both of you."

"Thanks. We're going to need it."

"What's he going to be when he gets out of college?"

"A veterinarian."

"Sounds like an interesting profession. You don't run into many of those. It's like running into a guy who's going to be a mortician." He fumbled for a cigarette in his pocket, brought it out and lit it. "What are you going to be majoring in?"

"I haven't really made up my mind yet. I was thinking of maybe agriculture or something. God knows, I know enough about it now."

Timmy wished he could tell her that her future husband could go straight to hell. He was jealous. But he would not show his feelings. You won't get anywhere, he thought. Except a fight. You could tell her you love her, you need her, you want her. But it won't do any good. It will only cause trouble. And why ask for trouble when she's calmed down to the point where you can at least talk to her. Maybe you could even talk her into supper somewhere. Keep walking toward the car. Then casually get in and say you're going to get a bit to eat and invite her. Casually.

He walked toward his car. And then he made his play. He stepped in and from behind the wheel, he invited her to come with him. Without a word of protest she accepted and he started the car and they drove onto the road that led into town.

It was a Mexican restaurant where they went. He didn't have much money, but the way he felt he was ready to spend every dime of it tonight with Nancy. It was, after all, an occasion to celebrate. Not so much her marriage, but their reunion. They had a big meal at the restaurant and afterwards they sat smoking cigarettes and drinking coffee while listening to canciones rancheras from the juke box.

For the most part, their conversation was on an impersonal tone. They were like friends who had met after being away for a long time, not like the ex-husband and wife who, upon meeting after a period of separation, talk of past events they had shared, past memories they both held for each other but didn't mention. Instead they discussed his car, how it had acted up last week. It had been the generator. And they talked about movies they had seen and about world events they had read about. In his mind though, he was loving her silently, inwardly overjoyed to be with her again, remembering the nights they had spent together. Warmly in bed on a cold evening after a hard day's work in the fields or in the groves. They had dreamed in those days as any young couple dreams, dreaming of what the future would bring for them. What they would do to mold the future their way. He would talk about buying a ranch and they would speculate on the number of children they would have. It was all so very customary for young people to dream, he thought. Now they would dream and build their lives on separate roads. It was funny how he never quite forgot her. Of course this would have been impossible. Just as it would have been impossible for him to stop loving her. And the nights he had passed without her, all lonely, all desolate. Even around the camp fires at night listening to the story tellers spinning their yarns, his mind was never with them any longer, but rather in a void of wondering where she might be. They had had a good life when they were together. In the evenings they sat around the fires, listening to the story tellers and listening to the guitars. Because there were always guitars. There was never a camp where someone didn't play the guitar. Since she had gone, he had fed the flame of his desire on the whores that were as much a part of the migrants' lives as were the unending crates of produce they filled out in the fields.

Before leaving the restaurant, Timmy insisted on picking up the tab. But Nancy had objected. She insisted that they go half-way on it. So after splitting the bill they left and drove back to camp.

Timmy drove deliberately slow. He knew that once back Nancy would disappear into her cabin and he would not see her until tomorrow. And tomorrow was a long way off.

"Does your knee still bother you?" she asked.

"Sometimes. Only in cold weather. Like always."

"Oh."

They were silent after this. The road they drove on was deserted. Fields of grapes passed them to either side. Timmy, while driving, was aware of the ghosts of campesinos between the furrows of the grape fields, translucent and slightly stooped, they moved slowly, haunting the land they had worked and never reaping anything more than a meager sum of what the land rendered. A land that, by right, should have been theirs. It was the same vision that came to him everytime he passed these fields. The grape fields especially; and these pellucid eidolons would sometimes be seen in the orange groves and in the peach groves. Occasionally, he would see them while he strolled through the fields, walking by them and through them as if he were walking through a fog. They were there. It wasn't in his mind. They were there as sure as he breathed the air around him. They were there. The men and women. The old ones and the children, too. Once, while driving down a similar road in this same region, he was with Acredano, an old campesino who had been drinking wine the greater portion of the day, who had turned to Timmy and said, "See them? Do you see them? They are there, like always. They are there." And Timmy looked and he thought he saw them. Although he was never quite sure what Acredano meant and somehow he was afraid to ask. But now, with the light of the moon flooding the area with silver light, he saw them. He was not mistaken. He saw them and he was sure that many other people saw them also. But one never spoke of it. It was simply an occurrence that was known among the workers and seldom discussed. It was a sight as unexplainable as anything metaphysical, as unexplainable as God Himself. This was a strange land. He knew this land as well as any migrant worker. It wasn't this land in particular. Any agricultural land held a certain kind of mystery which no other land did. It had to be a vast land, a land peopled by workers of the fields, workers that had dripped their sweat

on the earth as a testimony of having once been here, giving of themselves as most people elsewhere seldom give of themselves to their
occupations. Their forms were much like the auras that a psychic sees
around individual beings. These nonphysical entities were the lingering
souls of past migrant generations. There was one other such case which
Timmy thought of now, and that was the case of Old Samuel, a soldier
who had had an ear shot off during World War II. He had spoken of
similar experiences, though he did not tie it in with the phenomenon of
the fields. He spoke of the battle grounds in Europe and of the battle
grounds of the Revolution of Mexico and U.S. Civil War battle grounds.
He claimed to have seen the ghosts of dead soldiers walking around in
much the same manner that Timmy saw the ghosts of the migrant
workers in the fields. Samuel was a migrant worker who had a predilec-
tion for visiting historical battle grounds whenever he happened to be
near one, and he went there for the sole purpose of seeing what he
called the "floating spirits."

Funny that he never spoke of the ones in the fields.

"Timmy?"

He drove on as if he had heard nothing.

"Timmy!"

Startled, he turned, "Yeah?"

"What's the matter with you? I've been trying to get your attention
for the last mile."

"I was just thinking. Sorry."

"Look."

"What?"

"The ring. See?"

He glanced at her. There was a chain around her neck and on the
chain there was an engagement ring.

"Looks expensive," he said.

"It is."

"The guy must be loaded."

"Not really. He took it out on installments."

"I could never get you anything like that," he said. "I don't think
I'd want to. I'd just as soon put a cigar band around your finger."

"I don't know. I think it's kind of nice."

Momentarily and with some embarrassment, he recalled the brass
ring he had slipped on her finger the day they were married. The guy
who sold it to him, a jip in some novelty shop, had claimed the ring was
solid gold.

He knew it was too dark in the car for her to see him blush. Covering up his feelings, he said, "What's so nice about it?"

"The thought behind it. If a person's really in love and if he's willing to
show his love for you by getting in debt, well I think that's kind of nice."

"Well, it shows he's not stingy, anyway. But hell, if you think getting in debt is true love, well then maybe you should marry a pawnbroker."

"A pawnbroker doesn't get in debt," she said.

"That's right. He gets other people in debt. I suppose a pawnbroker gets in debt too, once in a while."

"I don't know. I've never been a pawnbroker."

"Neither have I."

"I don't think I'd want to be a pawnbroker," she said. "You make too many enemies."

"I've had my share of dealing with those bastards."

"I remember. It seems like out of season we were always pawning something."

They were coming to the camp's parking lot. When Timmy parked, he shut the engine off and neither made an attempt to get out.

"Well," he said, "we're back."

"Yeah. We're back."

They were quiet. They just sat staring straight out the window at the orange groves some yards ahead of the car, beyond the logs that kept the cars this side of the lot. Timmy took some gum out and offered a stick to Nancy. She accepted and they sat chewing, saying nothing. He thought that perhaps there was something on her mind.

He said, "Anything wrong?"

"No. It's just that it's been a long time."

"Yeah," he said. "It's been a long time."

"I'm sorry about this afternoon. The way I acted."

"Don't mention it."

"Timmy," she said, suddenly as if what she was to say had to come out rapidly. "I've never forgotten you. I never once forgot you. In fact, I still feel a lot for you. I always have. I guess I always will."

"You think there's still a chance then, between us?"

She was silent, thinking, running the question over and over in her mind. "No," she said finally. "I don't think so. Not after, well, him. I love him, Timmy. I really do."

"So there's no chance?"

"No."

"Not even one last time?"

She shook her head. "I can't. It wouldn't be right for him."

She was fiddling with the ring on the chain.

"Who's to tell him?"

"I can't," she said. "You know how it is."

Same old Nancy, he thought. Still as faithful as Mother Nature herself.

"So this is going to be your last season, huh?"

"Yep. After this season the only seasons I'll know will be the ones on campus."

"Getting back to civilization won't do you any harm, I guess."

They laughed and then he said, "We better get to camp. It gets early around here before you know it."

They came to the cabin area.

"Good night, Nancy."

"Good night."

He began walking away. Then she called him.

"Timmy, come here."

He went up to her and she kissed him lightly. Then she turned and walked in the direction of her cabin. He watched her walk away until she disappeared into one of the cabin doors.

Early the next morning, before anyone was up in camp, Timmy walked to his car with his suitcase in hand. He started up his car and drove away from the groves. There were plenty more farther north. He could get a job there just as well.

The early morning moon was still casting its light on the earth. As the car rushed down the road, he could see the phantom migrant workers in the grape fields. They seemed to be waving good bye to him as he drove farther away from where he had been.

WEEKEND

1

Gilbert kept scooping mud from a square patch of earth that resembled a miniature jungle. The moist earth was dug up with tediously built canals crossing and running into each other. The plot of earth was decorated, for the most part, with twines and small flowers and leaves and small islands of grass. Plants with thin stems served as trees. And Gilbert kept scooping. He was building a submerged flatland for his "good" troops. His "bad" troops were hiding behind some rocks about "five miles" away. Throughout the make believe battlefield there were trucks, tanks, jeeps, armed men, and even horses scattered about with other war machines. His armies were indiscriminately put together: contemporary fighting men, plastic cast soldiers fought alongside indians, King Arthur's Knights, and old time cavalry men. Gilbert was appropriately dressed in his playing clothes. He wore thin, faded levis and an army combat jacket with a Castro-type military hat. Gilbert kept scooping.

And Teddy wondered if he was for real. This wasn't the first time he had seen Gilbert. He had seen him often in the past, even before he had started going with Tina. However, every time, it never failed, he asked himself if Gilbert was really for real.

Gilbert was Tina's brother and he was sixteen years old. Teddy took his wallet out, flipped it open and took out a roach from the crevice where the wallet folded. As he toked in the roach he continued looking at Gilbert. Teddy was sitting on the front porch waiting for Tina. Gilbert began smoothing out the hole at the bottom and around the sides.

"You gonna do that all day?" Teddy asked.

Gilbert kept smoothing out the hole all around the inside.

"Ey, man. I asked you something."

Gilbert kept right on smoothing out the hole.

"What's the matter?" Teddy asked. "You don't like me or what?"

Gilbert lifted up his eyes to him and stared. He seemed to be looking through him. This gave Teddy the creeps. Man, the guy's a real nut, he thought.

A young brown boy came running bare footed across the street. The boy was about six and he wore a striped T-shirt and cut off jeans. His thin legs were streaked with dirt. He went up beside Gilbert and squatted down. Gilbert looked at him and acknowledged his presence with an agreeable smile, but said nothing.

"Can I play?" the boy inquired.

Gilbert nodded slowly and blinked his eyes.

Teddy wondered, while looking with puzzled eyes, if Gilbert had ever made a broad. Shit no. He probably didn't even think of broads.

To the young boy, Gilbert said, "Go get the hose from around the house."

The boy went and when he came back he was dragging a heavy black hose behind him. He held the muzzle over the small-like jungle and said, "Look at it rain, Gilbert. Look at it rain," and he turned the muzzle slightly, bringing down a sprinkling stream of water.

"Turn it off," Gilbert said. "I don't want it to rain."

The boy turned it off and handed the hose to Gilbert. He was going to fill his canals.

From inside the house, Teddy heard Tina say "good by" to her mother. He reached for his pack of cigarettes and took out a red which he had stashed between the pack.

"Give me the hose," he said, as he took it away from Gilbert. Teddy washed the red down and then handed the hose back. Gilbert hadn't said a thing and was now looking at Teddy like a reproached little boy.

"What's the matter?" Teddy asked.

"I don't like you," Gilbert said. "I want you to go away."

"Yeah," Teddy said. "Sure." Then he went back to sit on the steps.

"I told you I didn't want you here," Gilbert said, very much the mad little boy, pouting lips and all.

Teddy said, "Fuck you," in a heavy whisper and flipped Gilbert the bone.

"Come on, Teddy, let's go," Tina said. "It's already one o'clock." She came down the steps and Teddy got up.

Gilbert lent his attention back to his little island, pretending that Teddy and his sister weren't there.

"Wooooo!" said the little brown boy. "Look at that boat!" He was pointing to an ice cream stick that was floating down one of Gilbert's canals.

"It's a battle ship," Gilbert said.

2

The car chugged along. The car was getting hot. It was hot inside the car. He looked at Tina. It would start steaming in a minute. He had better get to a station.

"What's wrong, Teddy?" asked Tina, seeing the concern on his face. "Teddy, what's wrong?"

Everything. He couldn't fuck up the car. It wasn't his car for one thing, and without it he'd never be able to get his own car. He would need it for tonight.

"What's wrong?"

"Nothing," he said, pulling into a station. "It needs water."

Tina smiled. She was glad to know that the problem was so easy to solve.

Teddy got out and put water in the radiator. He held the hood up with one hand and, letting the water hose recoil into its cavity, stared at the engine of the car. He was up on weed and reds. Everything went real slow. Life was passing as a decelerated procession around him. What a trip, he thought, to look at the engine. He was fascinated by it.

The attendant came up with a friendly smile and said, "Can I help you with anything?"

Teddy looked at him and said, "No."

The attendant went back to his station in the office.

Teddy kept looking at the engine. This car was going to make him rich tonight. The engine looked oily, damp and yet warm, too, like a cunt that wants it. Then he thought of Tina. He would fuck her for luck, he thought. Put it good to her. Yes, he thought, yes. I'll fuck her for luck. He eased the hood down and got back in the car.

For luck.

"It was nice of your uncle to loan you the car today," Tina said.

He nodded.

"I like this day," she said. "Don't you like this day, Teddy?"

"Yeah," he said. "Yeah, I like this day."

He had other things on his mind. The park wasn't far from here. He'd take her to Elysian Park. There were ever hardly any people at Elysian Park, and even if there were it was easy to get lost there. Then, he thought, they might go to the Zoo. But after, only after.

For luck.

He swept the car around the curves as if he were racing it. He could hardly wait.

"Teddy, slow down. Stop driving so fast."

Teddy slowed the car down. Driving the car like that, fast, was like fucking a broad, he thought. It felt good.

He drove the car up the twinning road that led to the interior of the park. After following the road for some time, he turned onto a dirt and gravel lot that concaved in, off the road to near the cliff of the hill. Elysian Park is huge. The only thing that reminded one of being in the city was the smog.

From where he parked the car there began a path, a narrow path that led to the side of the high hill, onto thick ridges with trees and grass. Teddy looked at the path. That's where he would take Tina, he thought, down there somewhere.

"Let's get out," he said. "Bring the wine."

Tina grabbed the sack that contained the wine she had stolen from her father. Tina had come well prepared for their outing. In her suitcase-like purse she had a pink blanket so they could fuck in comfort.

As Teddy led the way to the path, he took a stick of weed from behind his ear and lit it. Nothing like the outdoor flavor. He took a few drags and passed it to Tina.

"Let's sit down there," she said, pointing to a grassy clearing where the sun was shining.

"No," Teddy said. "Let's see how far this trail goes."

So they continued walking down the narrow path that sloped down the hill and, finally, they came to its end. The path, at this point, was enshrouded in thick bushes. The center bush, rooted directly in the middle of the narrow path, was hollowed out, and inside this hollow of tangled twigs there was a haphazard bed laid out on the dirt floor. Beneath the soiled covers of rags there lay an equally soiled man, hairy all over and deeply tanned, almost black. He was like a balding bear in hibernation. Around the man there were wooden crates and cardboard boxes and two bottles of wine, empty bottles with no caps.

"I guess a bum lives here," Teddy said, looking at the man under the covers.

"Yeah," said Tina. "Come on, Teddy, let's go. I don't like it here."

"Let's stay," Teddy said. "It's a free country."

He stooped his head and walked into the hollow.

"Teddy, what are you *doing*?"

"Come on in. It's all right. That old man ain't gonna hurt you."

Tina stepped in with uncertainty and Teddy got two crates and they sat on them at the man's feet. The man didn't move. It seemed as if he weren't even breathing.

"Ey, this is a pretty crazy place, huh?"

"Teddy, I think that man's dead."

"No he ain't. He's just passed out."

"I think we better go."

"Gi' me the cups," he said. He took the wine out of the paper bag and uncapped it. "I said gi' me the cups."

Tina took the cups out reluctantly, all the while looking at the man under the covers. Teddy poured wine into the cups and gave one to Tina.

The man under the covers didn't move.

"It stinks in here," Tina said. "Don't you smell it?"

The reds and weed and wine were beginning to kill Teddy's sense of smell. But he whiffed in deep and, yes, a vague scent of shit was very much with them.

"Yeah, I smell it."

"I think it's him," said Tina, pointing to the man under the covers.

"Yeah, I think it is," said Teddy.

"I don't like it," Tina said.

Teddy drank some wine and told Tina she should do the same.

The man under the covers moved, grawled and mumbled. Then he began to sit up.

"Teddy, let's go!"

"Stick around. Let's see what he's all about."

The man propped himself onto his palms. He sat with a drooping mouth and drooping eyelids, even his lower lids were drooped, so one could see the skinny bloodshot eye meat to almost the other side of the eyeballs. His eyes were yellowed and streaked with thin red veins and his lips were puffed and chapped. He bared his mouth back to stretch it out of sleep. Teddy saw the man's teeth. Every tooth in his mouth was decayed, crumbled to brown colored stumps sapped with wine. The man scratched under his arm pit and said, "What are you doing here?" to his visitors.

"Nothing," Teddy said. "Drinking wine. Want some?"

"You got wine?"

"Yeah. Wait. Pour 'im a drink, Tina."

The man rubbed his mouth with rough swollen fingers. The fingers were stained a brown-yellow with tobacco.

Teddy took the cup from Tina and handed it to the man.

The man grinned and said, "Thanks. My name's Ray."

"Glad to meet you," Teddy said.

"Yeah," said the man.

"Let's get out of here," said Tina.

"What are you doing here," Teddy asked the man. "How come you live here?"

"This is as good a place as any," said Ray, drinking his wine.

"What do you do? Eat worms or something?"

Ray looked at him and smiled. "Sometimes," he said.

"Don't you have no job or nothing?" Tina asked.

"I used to be a carpenter, by trade. Paid good, but—hell, I was looking for something better."

"Did you find it?" Teddy asked.

"I sure did," Ray said. "Here," and he patted the makeshift bed, raising puffs of dust around his hand. "Right here."

Teddy stared at the man who said he liked it there and felt like calling him a lying motherfucker.

"Weren't you ever married?" Tina asked.

"I raped my share of broads," said Ray, drinking his wine. "I'm all through with that, though. My new life don't lend no room for women. This is woman enough for me," and he raised his cup of wine. "Don't you ever get sick sleeping here?" Teddy asked.

"I'm fit as a fiddle," said Ray. "The only thing I have trouble with is my hemorrhoids."

The man who had once been a carpenter in his early years and who called himself Ray drank his wine and asked for another cup.

Teddy poured him another and another and another.

Finally they were all quite drunk.

Teddy was now thinking of making Tina. It would have been a groove if the man wouldn't have been there. He didn't want to screw in front of the man. Maybe they would go to the clearing up the path where the sun shone.

The man called Ray asked for another drink of wine. He drank it, laid back on his self-made bed, closed his eyes, smiled and began to snore.

3

The night was cold and fog hung in the El Sereno streets, thick, almost impenetrable. All the streets were silent.

"Turn your lights off," Peanuts said.

"Are you crazy?" Teddy said. "I won't be able to see anything."

"Don't worry. Just off the lights. We're going to park here and walk through the alley."

Teddy turned into the alley behind Hy's and parked the car on a dirt patch off the asphalt, next to the Legion Hall. The three of them got out of the car and began walking down the alley, making as little noise as possible. There were two alleys that came together like a T. When they came to the vertical they turned on it and were now walking parallel to Eastern Avenue, heading toward the liquor store that was midway down the alley. Their footsteps were grinding ill-sounding noises beneath their feet. As much as they tried to snuff it, the noise kept on as they walked. Peanuts whispered to Little Man, telling him to be careful when he was getting through the square inlet at the top of the back door. Little Man felt the tools at his waist. He had the hammer and the chisel and the crowbar. He had borrowed them from his neighbor just for this occasion. The three of them had checked the liquor store earlier that evening, the front and back, looking for the likeliest place of entry. They had all decided that the boarded up square above the backdoor was the weak point.

The store was sure to have a lot of money tonight, being Saturday— 3:00 in the morning, Sunday. The three of them imagined the safe piled high with crisp bills. They had all seen the safe at one time or another

when they went in to buy gum or cigarettes. This was going to be easy.
Little Man and Peanuts looked scared. But, thought Teddy, no more
scared than he was. Only this was going to be easy. They would bust in,
bust the safe and make it with the bread. Easy. Simple. No mistakes.

When they came to the back fence of the liquor store they stopped
and looked at the square patch of pine wood above the door. They
could barely make it out through the dense fog.

"Now you sure you know how to put out that alarm?" Peanuts
asked.

"Yeah, I'm sure," Little Man said. "I'm sure. The guy that told me
used to fuck with these things in his garage. It's no big thing. I used to
watch him mess with them."

"They're not all the same," said Peanuts.

"Stop worrying," said Little Man. He got one foot firm into the
chicken wire fence. Up he went. Two more steps up and he was over.

Teddy kept watch around the alley and at the still, unlit houses
around them. He couldn't see very far with all this fog around. It was
for the better, he thought. Everything seemed to be going their way.

Little Man climbed to the top of some soda boxes that were piled
up beside the door. Shit, the guy that owns this place is just asking for
it, Teddy thought.

Peanuts kept looking at Little Man, and then around into the fog as
Teddy was doing, wondering if the cops would come by suddenly from
the fog, or if anyone from the houses was looking at them at that very
moment, dialing the law. It became very cold all of a sudden, far colder
than the weather was and Peanuts shivered.

Over and over again they kept reassuring themselves: It's going to be
easy knocking off a chickenshit place like this. But they had never
knocked off any big job. Petty theft, joy riding, house burglaries. This
was the first time they were going to try a liquor store with an alarm.

Little Man worked on the wires inside the box, carefully feeling his
way from one wire to the next. The guys below wished to hell he'd
hurry up and get in. So far the alarm had been silent, but just in case,
the guys standing watch were ready to run if anything went wrong.

Little Man tied the last two wires in the box and then tried opening
the boarded up square above the door. After a few solid shoulder
pushes the board collapsed. He went in, and only after he was half way
in did he turn on the flashlight. He could see the safe from where he
was. Little Man climbed all the way in and jumped to the floor. Peanuts
went over the fence and then Teddy went over. They went up the soda
boxes, then into the square hole and finally down to the floor of the
liquor store. Little Man was running around the main section of the
store filling his pockets with candies and gum and cigarettes.

He said, "Hey, we got this place all to ourselves." He was all smiles.

Peanuts picked up the tools that Little Man had left by the safe and began hammering on the dial. He tried it first with the hammer and then with the chisel and then with both. The damn thing wouldn't open. Then Teddy tried it. First with the hammer and then with the chisel and then with both. Nothing happened. All he managed to do was to put dents into the steel dial and around the safe's door.

Peanuts called Little Man, who had since gone and helped himself to some beer. He held an open can and he offered the rest of the pack to Teddy and Peanuts.

"Later," Peanuts said. "We can't get this thing open, man."

"Let me try it," Little Man said, taking the hammer and chisel. He began pounding on it with one, and then the other, and then with both. The safe kept steady, suffering only minor nicks. "Maybe we can take it with us," he said.

"You're nuts," Peanuts said. "That thing weighs more than all of us put together."

"What we gonna do then?" Little Man asked.

"Make it," Teddy said. "The law might be here any minute."

"We just got here and already you want to leave," Little Man said. "We got the place all to ourselves. Let's stay and dig it."

He opened some beer cans for Peanuts and Teddy from the sixpack. Then, as they drank their beer, they began ransacking the place. They found some change in the cash register and split it. Then they began putting candy and whiskey bottles and cigarette cartons into some potato sacks they found in the broom closet, stuffing their pockets as well. From the large front window they saw the fog licking itself against the panes. The street was deserted.

When they finished the beer they opened a fifth of Johnny Walker, mixing it with 7-Up. They poured half the soda out on the floor and poured the Johnny Walker in. They sat next to the safe with their potato sacks filled. There were four potato sacks and each one was filled to capacity.

"Shit," said Little Man. "We didn't do too bad." He flicked the ashes of a Hav-A-Tampa next to the potato sacks. "We can sell this shit and still get some bread."

"Ey, that's right," said Peanuts.

"I wonder how much is in the safe," said Teddy.

"All kinds, I bet," said Little Man.

They looked at the safe again as if it were a virgin girl resisting their charms.

"Fuckin' safe," Peanuts said.

"Goddamn it," said Teddy. "If we could only get into it."

Little Man said, "I bet there's a thousand dollars in there."

They eyed the safe with drunken stares. Peanuts picked up the hammer and began pounding at the dial again. Harder . . . Harder . . . HARDER! Nothing happened. The safe remained unmoved and indifferent.

"Fuck it," said Little Man. "Let's get this shit and get out of here. We ain't gonna get that thing open."

Little Man climbed to the square over the back door. They tied the potato sacks with string and between Teddy and Peanuts they lifted the sacks up to Little Man. One by one, the sacks went out of the liquor store until they were all lying by the soda boxes. Then they found themselves with four sacks behind the chain-link fence.

"How we gonna get them over?" Teddy asked.

The three of them studied the situation. It hadn't been too difficult getting them out of the store. Once they were out of the square, Little Man had simply propped them up on top of the empty soda boxes, hopped down and eased them down to the ground. But now they faced a problem. They couldn't very well balance the sacks on the fence.

Then Peanuts said, "I got it. Get on the other side of the fence," he told Little Man.

Little Man went over the fence.

"Okay," Peanuts said to Teddy, "I'm going to get on top. You hand me the sacks and I hand them down to Little Man."

Teddy nodded and Peanuts perched himself up on the fence.

"Start handing me the sacks," he said.

Teddy lifted a sack up to Peanuts and, in turn, Peanuts slid it down to Little Man. Then the second sack went up and over, and then the third. Teddy began to lift the fourth sack up when Peanuts suddenly yelled, "COPS! RUN!"

The sack came down full weight on Teddy. It crashed to the ground, soaking him and the asphalt with whiskey. He stood and scuttled up the fence, jumped down and fell, scraping his knee.

"Stay where you are or I'll shoot!"

Teddy heard Little Man's and Peanuts' footsteps echoing over the parking lot, and then over onto Eastern Avenue.

"Hold it right there!"

They were getting farther and farther away. Teddy began running, following them.

"STOP!"

Then the shots were heard, cutting into the fog.

4

Summer time. Sunday morning. The sun glowed hot and threw a blinding glare over the neighborhood streets. Gato was walking down Eastern Avenue, heading toward Wilson High, when he saw Freddy coming out of the Mexican bakery just next door to Mama Gloria's

Pizza Parlor. Freddy was munching on a huge piece of Mexican sweet bread shaped like a pretzel. He was by himself, which was kind of a surprise. For over a month now he and Big Hugo had been hanging around together like a couple of Siamese twins. The reason being that Freddy had been jumped by a gang from the Eastside while walking his girl Vera home from a dance. Beat the shit out of him. Vera ran screaming for the law. But by the time they got to him he had needed fourteen stitches on his head and a cast for his left arm.

Freddy still wore the cast, and as yet his hair hadn't grown completely out from where the stitches had been. You could still see the red, smeared iodine on his scalp. The scar beneath the bald patch looked nasty. It humped over like a grafted worm on his head. As Gato approached him, Freddy greeted him with his goofy smile that allowed one to see the gold caps on his front teeth.

"What's happening," Gato said.

"Nothing much," Freddy said. "Just standing around."

By now his cast was signed by just about everyone that knew him, and by many more who wouldn't remember what he looked like if he were standing on the line up. He had fallen into the habit of asking everyone he met to put their mark on his plaster, and for this purpose he carried a pencil behind his ear for anyone who might care to register their name on his arm. The cast served as a novelty for him; and it was apparent that the cast had inflated his ego to some extent. He displayed it as if it were a symbol of his savageness, even though he hadn't been much of a savage when he earned it. Still, Freddy waved the cast around like a medal.

Shortly after he got jumped he sort of picked up Hugo to walk around with him. A bodyguard wasn't a bad thing to call Hugo—in Freddy's situation, anyway. Freddy latched onto Hugo and managed to keep him at his side by treating him to cokes and things when they were on the street. Today, though, Hugo wasn't with him.

"What happened to Hugo?" Gato asked.

Gato suddenly got the feeling that he had put Freddy on a bummer. His goofy smile vanished and on came this
WHAT-THE-FUCK'S-THE-MATTER-WITH-YOU
type look.

"I don't know," he said. "I ain't seen him around."

Gato thought he detected a hint of anger in his voice.

"How's your arm?"

"It's okay."

"That's good, man. Hope you get over it soon."

"Yeah." He had that sound in his voice that suggested not wanting to continue the subject. Then he said, "Have you signed it yet?"

"A long time ago. When you first had it put on."

"That's right, I remember." He began looking for Gato's name on the cast.

"You got a lot of names on it," Gato noted.

"Got a lot of girls' numbers too." Freddy's smile came back. His mind was off his troubles.

"What does Vera say about it, man? About the numbers? Doesn't she get pissed off?"

Freddy's eyes became sad and his smile diminished to a faint grin as Gato watched the corners of his mouth twitch.

"She broke up with me a few days ago."

"That's too bad, ése. I thought the broad really dug on you."

"Naw, man. You know how it is."

Freddy munched on his sweet bread and chewed slowly.

"Ey, Freddy, did you hear about the dude they gunned down at the liquor store?"

"No. Who was it?"

"I don't know, man. But they got the dude's blood all over the street."

"Cold shot," Freddy said.

They went and sat in the shade of the Pizza Parlor, on the red brick wall that rose up from the walk. Inside, Mama Gloria was making ice tea for a girl and her mother. The girl was about ten and she wore green tight shorts. She had a well cushioned ass. Her legs were summer tanned. No one else was in the parlor. The young girl looked good to Gato. The passers-by on the Avenue were dressed in clean Sunday clothes, some coming from church, others going. Cars passed with families scrubbed and polished for the Mass, for Kingdom Hall, or whatever. Lowriders passed on their way somewhere to get loaded, to jug, drink and get doped up.

It was a happening Sunday.

"Did you go to church today?"

"Yeah. Early this morning," Freddy said. "I go to church every week."

"You're bullshitting," Gato said.

"No I'm not. It makes me feel better. After church I have all week long to fuck off and sin all over again. Vera and me used to go every week. She's very religious." He bit into his sweet bread, looking out at the Avenue, watching two girls across the street walking and shaking their ass like made up dolls. Freddy was smiling again. Gato began to wonder why Vera had broken up with him. But then, of course, it was none of his business.

"What did you do last night?"

"Nothing much," Freddy said. "I tried to get the guys to go looking for the punks that—" He stopped abruptly, not wanting to finish what would end as "jumped me." It was painful enough as it was, that everyone knew of it. No sense in reminding them. "Anyway," he said, "no one wanted to go. Everyone's chickenshit when it comes to helping out a friend."

"They just don't want to get into it," Gato said. "No one wants to hassle in the summer."

"Bullshit. Those motherfuckers are just chickenshit, that's all."

"Why don't you let the guys know how you feel about it, man. I'll tell them if you want."

"I don't give a fuck," he said. "Go on, tell them."

Gato felt like blowing his mind.

"What if they come looking for you," he said. "They're liable to kick your ass all over again."

"Hell they will. I'll tell them to their face. They're chickenshit!"

Gato shined him on. Freddy was just blowing wind.

He looked at the green wall of the bakery. It was covered over with names and symbols. Gato had his name on the wall: El Gato de La Happy Valley C/S. So did Freddy. Then he noticed that another couple had been added. To Gato's surprise, the announcement read:

EL BIG HUGO
CON
LA VERA
C/S

Gato wondered if Freddy had seen the declaration yet. Then he saw the lead pencil arrow pointing to Hugo's name. At the end of the arrow the word PUTO was written. Gato had no doubts then that Freddy had seen it.

When Gato turned back to him, Freddy had his head bent, looking at his half eaten sweet bread. He knew that Gato had seen what was on the wall. Gato didn't say anything or want to stick around any longer. With his good hand, Freddy rubbed the cast on his arm and then scratched the scar on his head.

"I'll see you later, Freddy. Take it easy."

"Where you going?" he asked.

"To the park."

"You gonna watch the broads in the pool?"

"Yeah. Smoke a little weed."

"I'll make it down with you," he said.

"Sure, man. But what if the guys are there?"

Gato wondered if Freddy knew what he meant.

"Ain't no big thing," he said.

They started walking down the Avenue again.

5

The El Sereno Playground brimmed with Sunday visitors. People were picnicking at the tables and little league baseball teams were out in the field. The swimming pool was filled, and bronze lifeguards sat in high stilted chairs watching over the people. Broads and dudes lay stretched out sunning themselves, laughing, playing, swimming, diving, wading in the pool.

Up on the elevated portion of the park, where the four logs squared in the fire site, lowriders sat around talking about last night's shooting.

"They cut him down without any kind of warning," Little Man said. "Those cold blooded motherfuckers shot him down like if he was some kind of dog or something."

"How do you know?" Bennie asked. "If you guys were too busy running, how do you know?"

"We know, man, we know," Peanuts said. "You know how cops are."

"No lie," Tony said. "If you're a Chicano you're a dead man as far as they're concerned. My old lady wanted me to call the cops on Mike because he ain't showed up at the pad. But shit, I said later. I ain't gonna get no cops on my brother."

"I wonder what Tina's going to say when she hears about Teddy," Peanuts said.

"I don't know, ey," said Bosco. "But there's all kinds of other dudes. She ain't gonna be lonesome for long."

"I'd like to pick up on that broad myself," said Little Man.

"I got into her once," Bennie said. "She's good pussy. She knows how to make it good."

"I'd like to feed her some myself," said Tony.

Peanuts said, "Is she tight, Bennie?"

"She's okay. Tight enough, you know."

"You think Teddy's people know about it yet?" said Bosco.

"Yeah," said Peanuts. "They probably know."

"I bet his old lady wet the floor when she found out," said Little Man.

"Your old lady would too," Tony said, "if some cop gunned you down."

Little Man said, "You think the law is still looking for us?"

"Shit yes," said Bosco. "There's all kinds of heat cruising the neighborhood. They just keep going up and down the streets like if they're looking for something."

"Motherfuckers are just wasting gas," said Peanuts. "They ain't gonna catch us."

"You think they'll take prints," asked Little Man.

"Shit yeh," said Bennie. "They always take prints."

"Fuck it. I ain't gonna let them take me in," said Little Man. "They got to shoot me like they did Teddy before they take me in."

"And they'll do it too," Bosco said.

"Hell yeh," said Bennie.

"Fuck 'em in their ass," said Little Man. "If they want me, they're going to *have* to shoot me."

Down by the dirt and gravel parking lot, a squad car stopped and the cop got out to talk to two guys that were coming up to the park.

"Who is that?" asked Little Man. "I can't see too good."

"Looks like Gato and Freddy," said Peanuts.

Bennie said, "Yeah, that's Freddy. I can see his cast."

"I wonder what the cop stopped them for," Tony said.

"Just to fuck 'em around," said Bosco.

"Maybe the cops want to know about Teddy," Bennie said.

The cop appeared to be writing something down on a piece of paper. Gato and Freddy nodded at times and at times shook their heads as if answering to the positive and the negative. Finally, the cop got back in the squad car, turned around and drove back to Eastern Avenue.

"Lousy motherfucker," Peanuts said. "For two cents I'd shove a turd in that bastard's face."

Shortly, Gato and Freddy came up to join the other guys, and Little Man said, "What'd that cop want?"

"He asked us what we were up to last night," answered Gato. "And then he asked us about Teddy."

"If we knew him and shit like that," said Freddy.

"What'd you tell him?" asked Peanuts.

"We told 'im yeah," said Gato. "What the fuck's going on anyway?"

"Did you hear about what happened at the liquor store?" asked Tony.

"Yeah," said Gato. "Some dude got shot."

"It was Teddy," said Little Man. "Some cop shot him."

"You swear to God!" said Freddy.

"No bullshit, ése."

"I don't believe it," Gato said. "What the fuck happened, man?"

Little Man began telling him what happened. The guys talked about it late into the afternoon.

CUTTING MIRRORS

It was ten o'clock in the morning and Anthony Alonzo, advertising copy-writer who was "ditching the dungeon" for the day, sat under a willow tree on a green matted hill reading a book of poems. His face was intent and at times, depending on how the poem struck him, he smiled or chuckled. He had been there since eight-thirty, and for the sake of self-expansion he had brought half a can of grass with him. At nine o'clock he rolled and blasted his first joint, and now he was undecided as to whether he should continue reading Housman or to eat lunch. It took him only a moment to decide. He would smoke another joint and read five more pages and in the end have a greater appetite than before.

Another hour passed and, after lunch, he lit two more joints and soaked in page after page of poetry. By eleven-thirty his mind was thoroughly clouded in grass smoke and his last page of poetry was turned. Now he was thinking of the drive to the country. He had hummed and looked at the oaks and pines and he left his senses free to entertain themselves on the fragrances of the environment.

. . . long drive from the city . . . smoggy . . . dusty . . . hum and purr . . . engine beneath the hood . . . music to nowhere special. . . .

The autumn leaves and trees were blowing and swaying gently around him. The slow motion of marijuana made everything calm. The sky was a sheet of resonant blue, deep in tone, and clouds were being swept east by a strong breeze. The rolling fields of grass were augmented by mottled stretches of flowers to the east and south, and to the north and west golden fields of alfalfa and wheat covered great terrains. The rustling branches and the sound of the wind and the leaning of high grass had Anthony mellow-minded and he could almost see Athena running up the hill toward him, a white bandana over her brown hair and wearing a full, plain dress pressed by the wind to her body.

. . . past twelve now . . . they're having lunch at Francisco's. Martha's sitting in her corner on her huge bottom, gulping a pitcher of beer and sinking her teeth in a pizza. . . . Harold picking his spaced teeth, drinking chocolate Metrecal . . . making squinted eyes at every female passing his way. Old lady Lowlinn, scratching her wiry grey hair, dunking French bread in a bowl of beef soup . . . reading the ads in the L.A. Free Press. . . .

. . . traffic and lights . . . floors and more floors . . . air-conditioned sweatroom in which to think for the machine that spits out the check every other week . . . the boss, that glowing creature . . . disgusting to look at his phosphorescent smile as he says: "Get this out fast enough, Tony, and we might consider giving you a raise."

As far as Anthony was concerned, the ads could wait. At this point in the day he didn't care whether he lost his job or not. The moment, this moment, was enough for him. The mere thought of feeling cleansed from the city ways, and the ways he functioned in the city, had him at ease in a way he could not have felt in L.A. The air was clean and fresh; away from smog, he felt alive. All thought that came his way was welcomed. This mood was felt by every sense and cell, giving him knowledge of being Man rather than counterfeit *Homo sapien*. In this and in many other thoughts he drenched his mind, gliding from mood to mood, not caring for answers, just for a moment of wholeness.

Athena, the only one he cared to think of, was the waitress at Francisco's. She wasn't tall like the models in the pictures for which he wrote captions. She didn't have to be. She wasn't skinny and she wasn't fat. Her breasts were large and robust, and there was a flush in her cheeks that were dotted with almost imperceptible freckles; and her thighs were of the bulging kind that he enjoyed smothering into on a winter's night. No warmth on a cold evening could be so sensuous or rich as that of Athena's thighs. She was vain, but justly so. Her brown eyes were accented by shadows and thin black lines to illuminate the flick of mystery that dawned in them. Funny, he thought, that Athena could look so human in an apron. And again he imagined seeing her running up the hill to greet him, smiling and laughing in her way, running with outstretched arms.

With complete abandonment of reality, Anthony half rose and yelled a greeting to her; and, darting down the hill, laughing, he shouted: "Athena, I Love you!" and he continued running, bypassing her image and coming to stop at the foot of the valley, breathing hard and smiling at this jest of his imagination.

He looked at the length of the valley, and then he looked up at the hill where he had left his weed and book of poems. The leaves of the willow tree were waving to him in the wind. He sat cross-legged on the soft emerald grass and lit another joint. The drifting grass smoke mingled with the scents of Nature through the crisp air around him.

As he dragged the green smoke into his lungs he turned his head casually from one direction to another, seeing not a single sight of humans. Everything was the peace and calm of a country day, windy with white formful clouds. He had even gone to the trouble of parking his car some miles away. On days like these he wanted no machines or foul fumes in his way. He wanted no symbols to stifle the ways of his moods. He had left his tie and coat in the car, and his shiny shoes in exchange for the forsaken pair of loafers he wore. The seams of his loafers were torn and they were thoroughly sagged from their original form.

Because he wished, Athena's image appeared a few yards before him, more intensified than before, and he saw her features clear and telling of the woman that looked from behind child's eyes. He sat, smoking grass, with a faint grin on his face as he made a gesture to her to sit down beside him. She giggled and shook her head.

"Come on, sit down."

"No, I can't."

"Why not?"

"Because."

"Don't start that. Come sit down."

"I can't."

"Don't give me that. Now come on. Sit down."

"I'm not here."

"Then maybe you can tell me why I didn't bring you with me."

"Because you're foolish."

"I'm not either. Come sit down."

She shook her head and her image began to slowly fade as she waved farewell.

Thinking of her made him despair. She made him feel either too good or too empty. When he saw her in public he was hard put to restrain himself from looking too long at her. Even Harold had said that he looked at her in too odd a way, and what would his wife say?

Anthony began thinking, more solemnly now, about his wife. Lately he had come to regard matrimony as a masochistic bondage. That very morning they had fought at the breakfast table.

"Did you know that Peggy Ann's husband bought her a new wardrobe?" she said, looking at her bowl of Cream of Wheat.

He looked at her sleepy face and curlered hair.

"No, I haven't heard."

"He's making twenty thousand a year. Did you know that?"

"No."

"Well, he does."

"So what?"

"Listen you, don't get snotty with me."

"Who's getting snotty?"

"You are, stupid." Then: "I saw Danny Franks the other day. He got the new T-bird he was talking about. It's really a nice car. It rides so smooth."

She was quiet and watched him. When Anthony didn't answer, she said, "He asked me to go out with him."

"Really?"

"Yes, really. Want to know what I told him?"

"Not especially."

"Why?"

"You might tell me you refused."

"What do you think I am?"

"Does it make any difference?"

"You better take that back!"

He told her to shut up and she had laughed; he told her to shut her big fat mouth and she had spat her poison and she had laughed; he told her to shut her goddamn mouth and she told him to kiss her ass and she had laughed.

What kind of life was he living with Dorothy, anyway? They had been married for five years now. At first it was well that they had married. At the time they had both needed someone. But now they found themselves in other things. The sharp emotions between them had long faded, and whenever they did rise Dorothy had to be drunk in order to believe that she could love as she once had.

He could not suppress the distasteful things that were swarming through his mind. He thought of his wife and her dyed-hair friends, and he thought of his boss and his co-workers, and he thought of labels and values and signs and symbols and sticky products. His mind raced in a spin with ads and things of different shapes and sizes.

. . . spinning, spinning, spinning. . . .

And then, thundering from the clouds, came the Star Spangled Banner, and his mind spun and clotted and vomited every dollar sign out of his head.

In fright, he stood and began running up the hill. Then, in a sudden turn, he saw his nightmare in all its colors and dimensions a hundred times larger than life. In utter terror he saw a gargantuan roll of toilet tissue unwinding itself in his direction. It was coming from the northern horizon with such forceful speed that for lack of nerve he could not move. Then came this god-like voice, husky and deep, calling to him: "Sacrifice yourself, Anthony, to the Great God of Things!"

At the command Anthony ran as fast as he could up the hill.

"In the name of US and all Things in US, I command you to stop!" said the voice. "I will mummify you in my own image!"

In a sudden turn, Anthony stopped and saw the mammoth roll of toilet tissue still coming and getting closer. As it rolled it laid a carpet of pink tissue on which Dorothy made her way majestically with a Lady Lansoon Wig that dragged behind her, wearing nothing more than a kotex and a pair of rubber gloves. The Star Spangled Banner came louder, then louder; and from a fertileless field of crab grass and weeds the Stars and Stripes rose to the sky and took the shape of a massive eye, bloodshot and drooped with the letters CBS across it.

Glasses, thick as the bottom of a bottle of Coors, his teeth thrust an inch over his lower lip, and the upper barely making the cover, he saw his boss soaring through the sky perched on an eagle with a two cent price tag around its neck.

Then the most profound sight of all came.

In disbelief he saw everything on the commercial market charging at him from the eastern horizon. Every sales talk he had ever heard was at counterpoint with the National Anthem. He ran and ran up the hill, but the distance to the tree seemed an infinite journey. The army of Things kept coming, led by his wife and his boss who were making like geeks on Halloween and howling for his castration.

"Off with his balls!" screamed Dorothy. "Give me a man with sacks of lead and the mind of a weasel!"

The roll of toilet tissue spun and spun, and then as if from beyond his imagination there came a peace and quiet that left him with the sound of nothing in his ears. The fields were quiet and still. No trees stirred. No hum of bees or song of birds was heard. There was absolutely no sound of any kind.

At last, after what seemed like no time and all time put together, he heard his heart beating faintly. Harder and harder it pounded, drumming itself to a high booming crescendo, and then it ceased and was calm.

He stared at the horizon. Everything was back to normal.

He sat under the willow tree and relit the joint and wondered if perhaps he was going mad.

For the rest of the afternoon he sat under the tree smoking marijuana, and in his mind he skipped around looking through the recesses of his memory. More thoughts of Athena came to him. When the sun went down he would go for Athena, he thought, and he would bring her back to spend the night so that in the morning they could spend the day together.

BLUE DAY ON MAIN STREET

If I remember correctly, I had been a poet who had gone slowly insane, in a curable way, two years ago. I'm still not too sure about my name though. At the Institution they said I was a sex offender that was suffering from amnesia. They called me by many names at that place, and I responded to each and every one of them as if they were my true identity. Although, now that I think of it, they never called me a name I could fully respond to, as if knowing somehow that what they called me wasn't what I was, or am, or ever will be. To each his own, I always say.

The days at the Institution had been pink and red days for me. Except for the weekends; they had been toned many colors and shades, but not quite like the weekdays. I don't think I'll ever forget the little brunette nurse that came around to my room once a day, five days a week, pat me on the head and then grab my balls in either one of two ways. On red days she came in smiling with a joyful glee, ruffle my hair and then grab as hard as her little heart desired. Then again, on pink days she came in pouting in a kind of sorrow, or she would contort her lovely features in an angry grimace and, in either case, stroke my head and gently caress. Regardless of how she was in her handling I always received a perverse kind of pleasure in anticipation of her touch. For the better part of my stay at the Institution I passed my time thinking of the "outs" and wondering why the nurse enjoyed doing what she did everyday, five days a week. I could never figure it out. I once asked her and she slapped my face. I never asked her again.

Today is a blue day. Yesterday the doctor told me I was cured and to pack my bags and leave. I didn't have anymore to take with me than myself. And now here I am, back on the street. I made an effort to stay there, at the Institution that is. But no matter how much I tried telling the doctor I didn't feel cured, he wouldn't believe me and had me thrown out anyway. That's life for you.

Ever since I got off the Greyhound this morning I've been standing on 6th & Main in downtown L.A. taking in the sights. I could have gone to Steve's house after getting off the bus. I have his address. Three days ago, a red day it had been, he phoned me at the Institution and invited me to stay with him when I got out until I got back on my feet. How he knew I would be getting out so soon is beyond me. Anyway, it's a kind gesture. I met Steve at the Institution so I know I won't have any trouble getting along with him. Institution people are the easiest people to get along with, I always say. But I don't want to go there just yet. After all, it's my first day out.

As I look around me, I can't help thinking that what I see is just an extension of the place I left behind.

A tall lanky Negro on the corner is holding blue cards out to the passers-by. A woman with lavender skin puts a nickle in the tin cup and takes a card. She glances at it and then throws it away. The card says:

Pardon Me
I AM A DEAF MUTE
I SELL THIS CARD FOR A LIVING
Give What You Wish
THANK YOU

A hunchback with a whiffing white nose comes by and looks at the cards, and then he whiffs at the Negro's tin cup.

"I ain't got nothing to give," he says.

The Negro smiles.

The whiffing hunchback looks around furtively, blows some vapory air in the tin cup, takes a card and quickly walks down 6th St.

The Negro gives him the finger and shouts: "COME BACK HERE, YOU MOTHERFUCKER!" and then he runs after the hunchback.

Seething heat waves rise from pale walks. Cracked asphalt, soft tar oozing out of broken black veins. An erect landscape of concrete surrounds me. Windows kindle their shining visors with the reflecting blue sun. Passing people passing time, leaving their odors of sweet, cheap perfume to tussle my mind like a nickle bottle of port. Sweat stench and armpits and dirty cock and cunt. An old wino crosses the street and stops on the corner, waiting for the light to change red. His face is the color of manure and he resembles a dry fig. A Bull Durham sack sticks out of the shirt pocket. He leans against a lamp post, harks a jade oyster and blows it on the street where a lime colored cab is rounding the corner. He wipes the gummy excess off his mouth with the back of his hand. The light turns red and he slowly skids out to a magazine stand. Up the street, a man who's the spitting image of Farmer John is coming round 5th St. herding half a dozen hogs. Vigorously, he swings a black bull whip on their backs as he drinks vodka and curses his mother.

You find wholesome people most anywhere you go nowadays. As a friend of mine used to say, they're the ones that smilingly lie in your face and then cut your balls off while you sleep. I suppose he knew what he was talking about, for he did just that to some guy as the poor fellow was sleeping. Last July they had a massive manhunt for my friend. Only he got the better of them. He cut himself into little pieces with a straight razor before they could get their hands on him. He was a pretty sly character, that guy. As I understand it, he laughed and laughed as if he were being tickled to death while he sliced off layer after layer of his own flesh. Now that's a trick to learn. And why not? This guy even had the ingenuity to take pictures of himself showing his body all bloody and sliced to the bone. In one of the pictures he was holding up a strip of flesh and he was smiling. The pictures were given to the relatives of the victim he had castrated. I got to see them first hand from the victim's wife who was up at the Institution with me. It was something of a novelty with her, the way she'd go around showing them to everyone.

An old lady in a polka-dot mini comes by on rickety legs. Her mouth is coated with a magenta shade. Black mascara is smeared under her sagged eyes that well green tears. I smile at her, she smiles a wide open smile at me and a yellow tongue lashes out, hissing like a serpent. Albedo eyes roll as she passes. A green tear falls on the walk and her tongue recoils as I watch her body travel on down the block. From behind I see her bony figure rejuvenate into the plump body of a virgin I once knew. The voluptuous flesh moves teasingly as if aware of the swell it is causing me. Shoulders curve over naked, in a delicate, youthful way. She moves with a sway that makes me throb with each step she takes. An Indian pinches her ass and she turns into a fag bar and disappears.

At the Institution they said I was crazy. Seems like they never got tired of reminding me about that. Anyway, they may have been right when they said I was inconsistent with my life. But hell, who isn't?

Young and old faces. People dressed in every color you can imagine; from the style of the 20's to the mod look of now. A man with knobby knees crosses the street, going toward Broadway, with a soggy cigar in his mouth. As he walks I see his diaper giving heat waves off to the sun. Two queens in jeans walk by laughing at everything they see with large red eyes. Orange marijuana smoke lingers behind them. Across the street a teenage boy in soiled pink panties stands next to a Salvation Army group singing the Coming of the Lamb. The boy is selling white capsules for 5 dollars.

Here I am, 6th & Main, on the corner, caressing my hard-on with loving strokes. A teenybopper with blonde twat hairs on her head is standing dumb-mouthed at my side, staring at my bulge. I look at her and smile the smile I learned at the Institution. It's a rather stupid smile, but it keeps you out of trouble, or so they said at the Institution. They recommend it highly to all the patients there. If you see this smile on anyone you know right away that they've been to the Institution for some reason or other. It's not really such a bad place to be, I suppose.

After a while the Institution kind of grows on you. It can grow on you to the extent that when you leave you might get to feeling your days blue.

An old woman in mustard colored trunks walks by with a body over her shoulder.

"It's my son," she says, and continues walking.

There's a heart shaped bullet hole in back of the body's head. People pass, come and go. People watching people walk; people watching people waiting for buses. It seems that one learns to look and do little else around this place.

Above me the sun glares a bright blue. The sky is the color of blood. My pride shrinks. The light turns red, and I walk down Main, heading toward 5th St.

Juke box music is amplified from bars. Come the rhythms, slimy and sticky into listening oiled ears. Eyes shutter minute snaps of inner realities, reflecting perspectives to suit one's choosing. A middle aged woman with a cock and a pair of testicles just below her chin is lifting a pink poodle by its ears, smiling the Institution smile and saying, "I Love You," to the dog. Black shine boys shining shoes pop their rags with strips of tape across their mouths. Naked strippers' posters— PLAYING NOW & NEXT ATTRACTIONS—stare enticingly at horny eyes. Stale odors meet my nostrils as I pass open entrances to archaic theaters. With a green face, a woman of lard sits behind the box office reading a copy of Horseshit. She laughs and shows bare gums, and she wears a brass crown studded with plastic gems. I walk among the derelicts and see shabby women dribble their lust. Old ladies kneel in the gutter next to the Mission. Their feet caked with mud. Their hearts thumping, telling me they're two days away from death. Lost men look at them but do not see. A wino sits in a doorway like a dying saint, drinking his shortdog.

"Tokey," he tells me. "God never had it so good."

Neon lights are lit in red and pink and purple lights. All colors. Advertising Free Pussy and with each purchase *we give stamps*—any color—to paste your eyes open for the things in the catalog of your mind. Three swaggering Blacks come walking down the block, dressed in mod, wearing tinged shades and snapping their fingers to the jazz that's coming from a brown cloud above City Hall. A white man with an idiot's mouth comes by sprinkling coal dust on the street.

Life is pretty dull. There's no other way of putting it. Everything is bland and commonplace, just like my poetry. I've had nothing to write about. Nothing worthwhile anyway. All my poetry is full of cocks and cunts and little girls with dirty minds. My life has been pretty damn dull.

Anyway, now that I think of it, I went on a few acid trips before going insane, in an "official" way that is. When I was finally busted, I was caught red handed humping a lamb in a shed behind an elementary school. I was giving all kinds of hell to this beast (who apparently seemed to be enjoying it) when—BOOM!—like that these two cops are shining lights in my face. So like I was saying, I had been crazy way before taking acid, and even before I got busted. I don't remember when I went mad, exactly. I suppose it makes no difference. Most people don't remember when they go mad anyway.

Although, sometimes I wonder why I am crazy—if there's a reason for it.

I ask myself these questions every once in a while, not ever thinking I'll find any answers. But I still wonder about these things. I even tried telling the doctor at the Institution what I thought, and he said, "Abnormal delusions are common among your type."

ABNORMAL DELUSIONS! Get that! He even went so far as to say that what I saw around me was only in my mind. Well, I told him, if it's only in my mind then why is it that I see your head as a hardboiled egg giving off fart fumes? He had no answer for that one.

Here comes the bus. Steve should be up and around by now. He might even be jacking off. It's his favorite pastime.

The bus comes to a stop. The green mouth opens and the bus metamorphoses into a slimy bug with thin black legs. Before getting on I turn around and look at Main St. Everything has disappeared. The shop displays are gone; the magazine racks are empty. Cars and people, everything is gone. The slimy bug and I are the only things left on the street. Blue dust swirls throughout the deserted streets in small whirlwinds. The green mouth oscillates and sucks me in. I drop a dry turd down the driver's mouth and walk to the rear of the bus where an old man is sitting next to his corpse. The bus slowly creeps away . . .

TAMALE LEOPARD

I sat at the bar smoking a cigarette and drinking a beer. I had been there for fifteen minutes now. The bar was on Brooklyn, just off Soto. It was the first time I had been in this bar. Behind me men and women danced on the sticky floor to a loud Mexican tune that blared from the juke box, convulsing the hot bodies that slid and twisted in drunken rhythms. At the rear of the bar a group of men were gathered by the pool table shooting 8 ball. There was also a woman in that area of the bar. She sat alone at one of the small, round tables against the wall. She wore a leopard coat. From where I sat she looked youthful. Her hair was bobbed into a bubble form. I looked at her occasionally, wondering if perhaps any of the men shooting pool had picked her up yet. It didn't appear as if she were with any of them. She sat with a displayed look of detachment on her face. Like many of the other women at the bar, I gathered that the woman in the leopard coat was a whore. She seemed to be waiting for an initial approach. I thought it over. It wasn't a bad idea. I hadn't come to the bar to pick up women. But now that I thought of it, it wasn't a bad idea. I had nothing to lose. All she could do was refuse. There were other women who were alone, but the one in the leopard coat was the one that attracted me most. She would look at me and then she would look at the men shooting pool and at the ones who were against the wall watching the game. Maybe I was wrong. Maybe she was married. I looked at her left hand to see if she wore a ring. I could see that there was a ring on her finger but I was sure that it was not a wedding ring. It was too large to be a wedding ring and the ornament was a jade green piece of plastic. I looked at the men shooting pool. To go up and talk to her might prove to be embarrassing. It was easy to start a fight in a place like this.

A fat man in a soiled brown suit who sat at the next stool turned to me and said, "Putas. Todas. Take your pick." The fat man extended his hand. "My name's Pancho. Pancho Fuentes."

I shook the fat man's hand. It was sticky with sweat.

"Do you come here often?"

"No," I said. "This is the first time I've been here."

"Ah," he said. "Well, if you have come to find a woman then you have come to the right place. I've had just about every slut in here."

A dark, lean woman who sat on the other side of me gave the fat man a disdainful stare.

"What are you looking at?" the fat man said to her.

"You have a filthy mouth," the woman said.

"Look," the fat man said to me, "that whore sitting next to you is worth but two dollars, if that, and she insists on ten every time. You would have to be a fool to pay that much."

"Raúl!" the woman called.

The bartender turned in her direction and the woman motioned him over.

"Another one?" said the bartender.

"No," the woman said. "Throw that tramp out."

The bartender looked at me.

"The other one," said the woman.

"What are you up to now, Pancho?" the bartender said.

"Nothing," the fat man said. "Nothing at all."

"He's drunk and saying disgracing things about the women in here," said the woman.

The bartender gave the fat man a reproachful look.

"You better hold your tongue," the bartender told him.

"Raúl, you know that I say nothing but the truth."

The bartender looked at the woman. "Keep the truth to yourself," he said to the fat man. Then he went to get a beer for a customer who had just come in.

"My friend," the fat man said to me. "Do I appear drunk to you?"

I shook my head. Best to keep the truth to myself.

"Of course I'm not drunk. In all my days of drinking I have never gotten so drunk to where I don't know what I'm saying. I drink every-day, on the job and off. I make cheese for a living, my friend. We at Casa de Queso make the best cheese in the world. If I had some with me I would gladly give you some. To judge for yourself. Yes, I take great pride in what I do. And not only that, I am foreman there. Have been for the past ten years. The supervisors there have such high esteem for me that they even allow me to drink. So you see, I get a lot of practice. But I never drink to the point where I do not know what I'm doing. Nunca. I am a man of fair temperance, of modest tastes. My sole pleasure in life is to work for money and spend it on beer and women. Tell me, is there any better life than that?"

"No," I said, "I can't think of a better life than that," at once thinking of a dozen life styles I would have preferred instead.

The lean woman who had been sitting next to me and who had told the bartender to throw the fat man out was now dancing with a short Mexican to a bolero. The short man had a thin moustache and was like a slippery worm on the floor, exercising a set of steps that moved him from head to foot, making his legs appear as if they were made of flexible rubber. The woman on the other hand danced erect and stiff as if she had a board strapped to her back. They made a funny pair out on the floor. The woman was at least a foot taller than the short man with the moustache.

I turned to look at the woman with the leopard coat. She was looking down at her beer. Then she put her finger in the beer and began to stir it. She did this with concentration for a while before taking her finger out and licking it like a popcicle. Then she put her finger back in the beer and began to stir it again.

The pool table was empty of balls except for the cue. The man who had lost the game was now at the bar ready to buy the winner a drink. And the challenger at the pool table put his quarter into the coin slot and pushed it in. The balls came down in a noisy clamor. He put the rack on the felt and began placing the balls inside the triangle, putting the black 8 in the center. The woman in the leopard coat looked at the men around the pool table with a coy invitation on her face. But none of the men paid any attention to her. The challenger lifted the rack and the winner of the previous game stroked the cue ball, breaking the set-up and pocketing two "small ones" into the corner pockets.

The fat man finished his beer and called the bartender for a refill. The lean, dark woman who had been dancing came back and slid onto her stool. With her elbow she nudged me on the arm. I turned and found the woman giving me a toothless smile.

"What's your name?" she said.

I looked at her pink gums, well-washed with beer. She continued smiling at me unashamedly.

"Larry," I said, picking the first name that came to mind.

"My name's Rosa," she said.

"Rosa no es buen cosa," said the fat man.

Spitefully, the woman said, "Shut up!"

"Amigo, don't waste your time with her," advised the fat man. "Besides being toothless and ugly she will give you sores where you least want them."

"You talk too much," the woman said. "Eres cochino de maña y modo, cabrón."

"I'm only giving him a fair warning," said the fat man. "I should know. With what you charge and with the doctor's fee, you're not worth it, Rosa."

I began to feel uncomfortable sitting between the fat man and the toothless whore.

"Ha!" laughed the woman. "And for you I suppose I am not good enough. Look at yourself. A fat dog! You should see him eat," the woman said to me. "He is like a hog who has not eaten for a week, grunting and snouting, smearing it over his face like I put on make-up."

Ignoring the woman, the fat man said, "I will give you some advice, amigo. Use a rubber every time. For precaution. I have a few with me if you would like some."

"No thanks. I don't plan on using them."

"That is even better. A young man like you has no business in a cantina like this to begin with. Look around you. Everyone here is over the hill."

I glanced around the bar. The people dancing and sitting at the bar and tables all appeared to be over thirty-five. I was by far the youngest one there.

"You see," said the fat man. "Everyone here is on the make. To get something from one another. I don't believe you're here for the same reasons."

I looked at the woman in the leopard coat. The fat man was right. I hadn't come here with any idea of picking up a woman. I had gone out of my apartment only for some relaxation and a drink or two. However, I was now thinking seriously of approaching the woman in the leopard coat. She seemed so apart from everyone else here, as if she were held in an invisible cast of isolation. This somehow attracted me. I was here and she was here. And I had nothing to lose. I was sure by now that she was completely alone. None of the men playing pool or looking on made any attempt to speak with her. I turned to the fat man.

"Who's that woman over there?" I asked.

The fat man looked. "I don't know. I've never seen her before. Pretty though. Why? You want her?"

"I was just asking."

"Well, better take her before someone else does. Material like that doesn't last too long in a place like this."

I motioned for the bartender, ordered two beers, and then went over to the woman's table.

"Anyone sitting here?"

The woman looked up and stared at me with what I interpreted as suspicion. Two of the men at the pool table were looking at me with not too friendly expressions. Her boy friends, I thought. Maybe. Maybe not. I stood there with the two beers in hand, looking at the woman.

"What do you want?" she said.

The question was blurted at me with a tone of irritation.

"Well," she said. "What is it?"

Feebly, I said, "Nothing," pulling out a chair to sit down.

"I didn't say you could sit down," the woman said.

"I thought maybe you'd like some company."

"I don't," she said.

"Here. At least share a beer with me." I put the glasses on the table as a sign of good will.

"Maybe you didn't hear me," the woman said. "I said I didn't want any company."

I ignored her and poured beer into my glass. I somehow got the feeling she was putting me on.

"Listen," she said. "What do you want?"

"Nothing. Just thought I'd come and talk to you. I saw you sitting here alone and I thought that maybe you were lonely."

"I'm not. I like being alone."

"At least let me finish my beer," I said. I took the other bottle and poured beer into her glass. The woman watched the glass fill until a crown of foam covered the yellow liquid. When I put down the bottle the woman picked up the glass and, without drinking, seemed to be whiffing at the brew.

"You didn't put anything in it, did you?"

"You saw me pour it."

"Well I don't know. Maybe you had the bartender put something in it."

"Like what, for instance?"

"Drugs. I know about those things."

"From experience?"

"No. But I'm not stupid. I know about those things."

"Don't worry. I didn't put anything in it."

"A girl can't be too careful."

"Sure," I said. "I understand."

The woman took a sip. Then she put the glass on the table and stared into it. We sat there, not saying a word. I listened to the loud music amplified to the point where the talk at the bar was like indistinguishable squawking to my ears. The billiard balls were clicking and rolling hollowly down the pockets. The fat man at the bar had now moved over next to the toothless whore. They were laughing loudly and the fat man's shoulders were shaking up and down in quick beefy motions. The toothless whore covered her mouth with a boney brown hand as she laughed.

"Do you live around here?" I asked the woman in the leopard coat.

"Yes," she said. "That is, no. I mean, I don't know."

"You don't know where you live?"

"Of course I know where I live."

"Then you do live around here."

"Yes and no. It's not too far from here."

"What's your name?"

"What do you want to know for?"

"Just asking."

"Well, it's none of your business."

This one's really weird, I thought.

She was smiling at me coyly, like a girl. A very young girl. Her brown eyes were trying to flash a spark of innocence at me. Her dyed black hair was like black string.

"My name's Esther," she said. "What's yours?"

"Alfred," I said, this time telling the truth.

"You look familiar," she said. "Have I seen you somewhere before?"

"Could be. It's a small world."

She gave me a penetrating look as if she were trying to recall my face.

"I know I've seen you before," she said. "I just can't remember where."

Esther was an attractive enough woman. Although there was a strange quality about her that not so much frightened me as it made me wonder about her. Why is a woman her age playing the part of a young girl, I wondered? Well, I thought, I had gone this far, so now there was only one thing to do. To get her into the car. I looked at the clock. It was 12:45.

"Do you come here a lot?" she asked.

"No. It's the first time I've been here."

"It's the first time I've been here, too. It's nice here. Don't you think?"

"It's okay."

The little girl attitude was everywhere on her, in her manner of speech and in her facial expressions. I couldn't tell if this was an act or if this was her true self. If it was an act, she did a good job of it. If I would have closed my eyes and listened to her I would have been listening to a sixteen year old girl. Now, as I looked at her, I wondered how old she really was. Thirty, I thought. At least.

She sipped her beer. "Are you married?" she said.

"No. I'm too smart for that."

"I wish I were married," she added.

"Why don't you get married then?"

"No one'll marry me."

"I can't see why. You're good looking," I said. Then thought, and added, "Young."

"Really think so?"

"Sure."

"How old do you think I am?"

"I don't know. Twenty-five, maybe."

"Wrong."

"How old are you?"

"Twenty-seven."

I knew she was lying.

"You look younger than that," I said.

"That's what everybody says." She looked down at her beer.

"What are you going to do when you leave here?"

She looked up. "Go home," she said.

"Do you live by yourself?"

"Why do you want to know?"

"Curious."

"Yes, I live alone."

"What do you do for a living?"

"I'm a secretary."

I was running out of questions. I wasn't accustomed to picking up women in bars.

"Have you got a car?" I asked.

"No."

"How did you get here?"

"I walked."

"I can give you a ride home if you like."

"Okay. If it's not too much trouble."

"No trouble at all."

We had a few more beers before leaving. On the way out the fat man noticed me with the woman in the leopard coat. He came up to me. "Here," he said, and he put a prophylactic in my coat pocket. "Just in case."

Her house was modest. Duplex. Simply furnished. Portable t.v., record player. Worn, comfortable couch in the living room. Typical Eastside pad.

"You have a nice place," I said.

"It's no palace. But I'm happy."

It had been no trouble getting in the house. I had simply asked if I could come in for a while. Sure, she said, why not. Want a beer? Yes, I said.

Now we sat on the couch. Esther was saying, "I feel good, don't you?"

"Good as ever."

"You think I do this all the time, don't you?"

"Do what?"

"Pick up men."

"I didn't say anything."

"Well, I don't. They pick me up."

I kept quiet and just looked at her.

"I know what you're thinking," she said.

"What am I thinking?"

"I can't tell you."

"Why not?"

"It's nasty."

"What's nasty?"

"What you're thinking."

"I'm not thinking anything."

"You are, I know you are."

"Okay. I agree. I'm thinking nasty things."

"What are they? What are you thinking?"

"Really want to know?"

She giggled. "Yes," she said. "Tell me."

"Really want to know?"

"Yes. Really. What are you thinking?"

"I want to go to bed with you."

"I knew it. I knew it."

"What?"

"Men are all the same. That's all they want."

"You wanted to know what I was thinking. I told you."

"I know. That's why I said that men are all the same."

"Okay. So now you know I'm normal."

"But you're so young," she said. "And I'm so old. You're nothing more than a boy."

"You're not old. You're only twenty-seven. That's not old."

"I'm older than that."

"Oh? I wouldn't have known if you hadn't told me. How old are you?"

"Too old. Too old to get married."

"You're never too old to get married. All you need is someone to marry you."

"I know. But Mr. Right just hasn't come along."

"Mr. Right will show up one of these days, don't worry."

"You wouldn't marry me, would you?"

"I can't marry anyone. I'm too poor to get married."

"What do you do anyway?"

"I'm a student."

"Really? I used to go to East L.A. College."

"I went there, too. For a while."

"It's a nice place. Maybe that's where I saw you."

"It's possible."

I had come to the conclusion that Esther was a dim wit if there was one.

"I can't go to bed with you," she said.

"Why?" This really shook me up.

"Because I'm waiting for Mr. Right. Besides I'm a virgin."

They all say that, I thought. "That's no excuse," I said.

"It's a good enough excuse for me."

"You should become a nun," I said.

"I've thought of it."

"Take your clothes off," I said.

"What for?"

"Just take them off."

"What are you going to do?"

"Never mind. Just take them off."

"I don't want to."

"All right. I'll see you. There's no reason for me to stick around any longer."

I got up and made for the door.

"Wait," she said. "I'll take my clothes off if you promise not to do anything."

"I promise."

She took her clothes off and sat on the couch. We sat there not saying a word.

Finally, I said, "Mind if I take my clothes off?"

"I don't care," she said. "If you want."

I stripped and we sat there naked.

"You must think I'm a whore."

"The thought never crossed my mind," I said.

"Good," she replied. "Because I'm not. I'm just waiting for Mr. Right."

I got closer to her. I could smell her. The bad b.o. dominated the smell of her perfume. Can't be choosy, I thought, and continued smiling. I knew I would never see her again after this. I was twenty-three and it was the first time I had ever picked up a woman in a bar. I had picked up girls before. The Eastside had two kinds of bars. Those for the young and those for the old. I had, up until tonight, patronized those for the young people. And like all bars, those who went to them went for companionship and to meet people, to meet them and, like the fat man said, to get something or to give something. Male and female. They were all in the same bag. And this happened to be one of those chance meetings. Where one met and then got lost, never to see each other again.

I put my arm around her and kissed her. Then we sat talking for a while. She said, "I'm tired. I'm going to lie down."

She stretched out and that gave me no place except to lie on top of her.

All in all, it proved to be an interesting evening.

FRANKIE'S LAST WISH

June, 1943. Los Angeles. Downtown Main Street.

Payaso walked with his crowd. The Pachucos were heading south on Main Street. The sailors were coming from the north. Spectators were on the sidewalks and on the street, following the two fighting groups from behind. This was it. Payaso was ready. In his right hand he held his switchblade, still folded. In his pocket he had a loaded .38.

The police were ready. Watchful observers. They were there only to clean up the remains of the battle.

The area was congested with people. Traffic was at a dead stop.

Payaso knew that his mother and his younger sister, Stella, were following in the crowd that fell just behind the zoot-suiters that were heading straight on toward the sailors. His mother had told him not to come. He would get hurt. He would go to jail. Or be killed like Loco from Dog Town the week before when some sailors pulled him out of a bar and stripped him of his clothes and beat and stabbed him to death while the crowd of on-lookers on the downtown street just watched. Like Loco, he thought, like Loco. But no; if he died now, he would die fighting. Like a man. Not like a victim. Not like Loco.

Payaso reached up to scratch at his left ear. There was a mole just behind the lobe of the ear. He watched the black wave of sailors advancing toward them. Closer. Payaso rubbed his thumb over the mole. It was a habit with him.

Pepe turned to him. "Payaso," he said, "watch it with them. They have cuetes."

It made no difference. Only now. That was all that mattered. Not an hour from now. Only now.

Pepe had a lead pipe in his hand. The other boys were armed with an assortment of weapons. Most of them concealed, to be brought out at the clash.

The sailors walked. The zoot-suiters walked. The crowd shouted, hissed, cussed and babbled over the scene.

"Dirty motherfuckin' Mexicans!" yelled a sailor.

"Chinga tu madre!" yelled Hector.

"Come on, greasers, we're waiting!"

"Fuck you in your ass, putos!"

The crowds watched as the two groups came closer to each other.

Mando said, "Payaso, I got one big surprise for those skinheads with this sawed off." It was concealed beneath his coat.

"Swing it like a bat when you unload it," Payaso said. "Make them count."

"Simón que sí, carnal."

Closer.

The sailors were ten yards away. Closer.

. . . *singing in the village square: the señoritas are passing by with roses in their hands.* Mando. The shotgun. He has a .22 in his pocket. Use it. *The rifle poised. The horse fell. A bullet in the head.* Closer. Hector. Shined his shoes all day for the fight. Spit. He could see himself in them. *The bleeding heart throbbing in the light of the flaming Sun. He won't die.* The people waiting, watching. Can see them through the corner of my eyes. Across the street. *A cross. He won't die. Drink the wine that will kill him for three days. Somewhere else; elsewhere again.* Alive again. Closer. *Heart beating in anticipation of the knife.* Closer. Alive. *In México. The desert heat. The sticky juice of the cactus.* In L.A. *In México.* On Main Street. The people, shouting. Wanting blood. Anybody's blood. Crowds of hungry flesh eaters. Eating with their eyes. Feeding what they feel with what they see. *Virgins.* The pace is slow. *Bleeding hands of blood.* Hector's shiny shoes. *She won't die.* Sweat gathering on my brow. *Damp climate. The spear, the fish, the spear and the miss and the warm damp climate.* Closer. They keep coming. *Sailing. What did they want?* Why this? *The gold. Plumed head-dress.* The dance last light at Cuco's house. *The feathers and the paint and the brown dancers dancing for the harvest.* Slow numbers got me hard against Virgie. *Wooden ships.* Closer. *Tall waves.* She was fine. Did it good. *Won't go back.* Fear. I feel fear. He's dead. Loco. Closer. *Won't die.* Got my gun. *The earth is quaking and the thunder of its anger devours. Man.* He called me a man. Then. The sailor the night last week said punk, greaser, dirty Mex. *The man of bronze called me a man.* Closer. The sailor. Told him to suck it. Fuck him. All the same. Killed Loco. *The furs and the cold and the meat and the rawness of it and the taste of blood.* Wine. Had wine before coming down. Warm now. Pato and his machete. Chop some head, Pato. Yesca was good too. *Two of them. Ripped out. I watched. Red flowers off a bush of flesh.* Richard said they raped his sister. *For survival.* I watch them coming. Closer. Coming and we going to meet them. To fight them. Warm and not afraid because it's too late to fear what is coming closer . . .

The first wave of sailors came on the zoot-suiters. Payaso was in the first file. The blade of his knife flashed open and he jabbed at the first sailor he met. The clash was like two tidalwaves coming against each other at once.

... ¡Revolución! The horses. The dust. The sounds of rifles biting the wind with their lead. The screams from the crowd. Hector's shiny shoes. The shotgun. Kicking in white faces. Laughing. Mando laughing. The shotgun scattering blood and flesh and bone over the street. Laughing louder than the burst of ... *Children go down under the fire of hot bullets ... Libertad, came the cry, ¡libertad! ...*

The swirling of aloneness that comes in battle came over Payaso. He knew only that he was in the center of a whirlpool of violence. His boys were on their own islands of battle. Drop kick and wide swings of his right arm, the arm that held the blade. It flashed past him into the neck of a sailor, ripping flesh and spurting blood. From behind a sharp pain entered his back. Payaso turned, swinging his blade.

... the wooden lance and the sharpened rock. The beast is crushing him and we can't do anything about it. Loco. He's dead. *And we try to kill the beast ...*

Now, he thought, now. He pulled the .38 out and charged into the black wave of sailors, firing bullets into the darkness of white striped uniforms. The rotating chamber, firing: one, two, three, four, five, six. Empty. Bodies falling. Zoot-suiters and sailors. Payaso clubbed now with the empty gun. His left hand ramming the blade into the sailors like driving a thick needle into black pin cushions. The blows and kicks and fists of brass knuckles came down on him from all directions.

... going back, going. They killed you, Loco. And I'm killing them and they're killing me. Going back, going back. The wall. The black wall. I can't make it, Loco. I can't make it ...

Gun shots boomed and sounded in the street, celebrating the death and violence of the moment. Mando was batting the shotgun and laughing like a man gone mad, cursing and yelling and telling the sailors their mothers were whores and he was laughing and enjoying the pain of all that was happening around him. Sailors retaliated with their weapons, their knives, their guns. Chains were swung and crushed against faces, leaving bloodied imprints and fractured bones. Screams from the onlookers came over the noise of battle, screams and shouts for more blood, for more death. Baseball bats came down on heads and across rib cages, and lead found its way into flesh and they went down under stomping feet, the dead and the dying. Those in drapes and those in uniforms. From building windows, people watched. From atop cars people watched. Neo-gladiators, in hate and defiance, in violent relentless destruction.

... the earth is quaking and the thunder of its anger devours ... he called me a man ... then ...

Payaso lay dead while the battle around him continued.

On the Eastside two people lay fornicating in a dark corner of an old house. Unaware of what was happening on Main Street, the man ejaculated with a sigh of pleasure.

April, 1970. Los Angeles. Eastside.
The house was up ahead. There was a street lamp on the corner. It was a large house, two stories high. Except for a light in the upstairs section, there were no other lights in the house.

The lowriding '58 Impala pulled up to the curb and parked. Nacho switched the headlights off and sounded the horn.

"Was a good geez," said Sammy from the back seat.

"It was all right," said Nacho.

"I've had better," Frankie said. He sat next to Sandra in the front seat. She was between him and Nacho. Since he had fixed he had been looking at the fresh needle mark on his left arm, putting his finger to his tongue and then dabbing it on the needle mark where the smack had entered his vein. He was feeling *muy loco* right now. While he dabbed at the arm he thought of making a play for Sandra. The guys had just picked them up on the Boulevard. Sammy had already latched onto the one in back. Now there was only Sandra left. But at the gas station, while the girls had gone to the head, Nacho had told Frankie that Sandra was his and to lie down.

Right now, the way he was feeling, Frankie didn't give a shit. There were only two broads and pretty soon there would be four dudes. Not enough to go around. And it was good looking pussy. Both of them. He thought of putting his arm around Sandra, just to see what Nacho would do. But, on second thought, it was best if he played his cards slowly tonight.

Everyone in the front seat was feeling good. So was everyone in the back. Only the people in the rear seat were feeling good in a twofold way. Sammy and Martha were in the back seat getting to know each other. Sammy pulled no punches. When they picked up broads like they had picked up Sandra and Martha, Sammy was the first to find out which one was ready and eager without playing the part.

"Looks like he ain't coming," said Frankie. "Give him the horn again."

Nacho gave three more blasts of the horn. The light from the upstairs section of the house went out.

Frankie looked back. Sammy was grinding and Martha's skirt no longer covered her thighs.

"Here he comes," said Nacho.

Someone was coming down the steps of the house. It was Aron. With a cool, sure Cholo step he made his way to the car.

"You people in back got to get up now," Frankie said.

"You're killing my kick," Sammy said. "I'm busy back here."

"Aron's got to sit down," Nacho said. "What do you want me to do? Put him in the trunk?"

"That's a good idea," Sammy said.

Aron opened the door and readied himself to step in the back.

"What you people doing?" he said.

"Making love," said Sammy. "What's it look like?"

"Save it for later," said Aron.

The couple sat up. Sammy pulled up his zipper and began combing his hair. The girl put her skirt back down over her thighs and, from her purse, she brought out a brush and began to tease her hair into shape.

Aron pulled the front seat forward and hopped in back. The girl was sitting between him and Sammy. Below the hem of the mini the girl showed solid brown legs beneath the skirt. The first pretty legs Aron had seen all day. He had not gone out of the house today, and the only legs in the house besides his own were those of his grandmother, thin wooden looking legs with thick and thin varicose veins running through them. Purple and green, ruptured and dilated. Nasty looking legs. His eyes were relieved to see the young and sexy legs of the girl that sat beside him.

Aron waited to be introduced to the two strange girls. But it appeared as if he weren't going to be introduced. The car was now moving toward Soto Street, down First. The windows of the car were down, all of them, allowing in the night air that rushed clean and cool over the people in the car. The radio was on. No one spoke. Frankie drank wine, and Aron wondered who the girls were. He took a Pall Mall out and lit it. Martha turned to face him with a coyness in her eyes and a playful smile. She had one of those lean, cat-like faces and her hair was disarrayed and teased high on her head. A pretty Chola, he thought.

Nacho took a joint from his pocket and lit it with the lighter of the car. Smoke began to rise from his goatee. Sandra was quick to snuff out the burning hairs on his chin.

"Be careful," she said, motherhood in every word.

Nacho passed her the joint. Sandra dragged on it and then passed it to the girl in back.

"We got some carga if you want to geez," Frankie said.

"Órale," said Aron. "Sta de aquéllas."

"Where can we go?" asked Frankie.

"To fix?" said Aron.

"Yeah."

"You got the outfit with you?"

"Yeah."

"We can cook in the car."

"That's too much of a risk," said Nacho.

"Can't go back to my pad," said Frankie. "My jefita's probably there by now."

Martha said, "We can go to my aunt's house."

"Does she fix?" asked Sammy.

"No," said the girl. "But she won't mind if we go there. You can use the bathroom," she said to Aron. "She won't know what's going on."

"Where does she live?" he asked.

"On Kern. Not too far from here."

"You want to go, Nacho?"

"It's better than cooking on the street."

On the way to Kern, Aron got to know the girls. Martha introduced herself and then she introduced Sandra. It didn't take Aron long to find out that the girls were already taken. Not for the rest of the night. But for the moment. It was better that way. Right now he wanted to fix.

The car came to Kern and Martha told Nacho where the house was. He parked.

"You want us to wait here?" he asked.

"No. Stella won't mind."

The six of them got out and went to the door. Martha knocked. From within the house it sounded as if a party were going on. Loud music from a stereo was giving the place a very lively atmosphere. Martha knocked again.

The door was soon answered. A woman in a robe stood at the door. She was slightly drunk and looked at the newcomers with laughing eyes.

"Stella," Martha said. "Thought I'd come to visit you. I brought some friends with me."

"Good," said Stella. "Instant party. Come in, come in."

Martha went in and the rest followed. The guys walked in as they walked in to all strange places: with caution. Like silent cats, they pawed onto the carpet, looking around to see if there was any adversary about. But the only other person in the house was a man with a bloated belly who sat at the couch with sweat beads on his brow like glass jewels. He had a thick, frowning moustache and a wide, hooked nose. He looked at them with suspicion. Beer cans were set on the coffee table, telling of the man's visit. He had been there a long while, for there were many empty cans around the room.

Martha's aunt stood in the center of the room in happy drunkenness, looking at the people who had just come into her house.

Then, suddenly, aware that a formality had to be taken care of, Stella, indicating the man on the couch, said, "This is . . . ah . . . ah . . . ?"

"Eduardo," said the man. "Call me Eduardo."

"Well," said Stella to her visitors, "sit down. Make yourselves at home."

Aron turned to Frankie. "Let's go to the head," he said.

"Where's your head at?" Frankie asked.

"Go through the hallway there," said Martha. "The first door on your right."

The guys went off so Aron could fix.

In the meantime, Nacho and Sammy and the girls sat down. There was a strain on the moment. Eduardo tried to look jovial. But inside he was afraid at the presence of the newcomers. He tried not to show his fear. But the feeling was there. Nacho sensed the bad trip the man was on. He gave Eduardo a penetrating stare, carrying it as far as he could, with a serious face, not letting his eyes stray in any other direction.

Martha, noticing the look he was giving her aunt's friend, said, "Nacho, would you like a beer?"

Without taking his eyes off the man, Nacho said, "Órale."

"Get me one too," Sammy said.

"You want one, Sandra?" Martha asked.

"Yeah."

Martha opened the cans from one of the six packs that lay atop the stereo and then she handed them to the people.

Stella said, "How's your mother, Martha?"

"She's okay. She's been wondering when you're going to come over."

"Never, tell her. You know I don't get along with her."

"You should come over once in a while. She worries about you."

"Oh, now that's a laugh. Her worrying about me."

"Really, Stella, she does."

"Well, tell her I will. One of these days."

"So how have you been?" said Martha, taking a beer and going to sit on the couch between the man with the bloated belly and Sammy.

"Oh, you know. Same. Working, drinking. Same old me." She swallowed some beer. "And you?"

"Nothing."

"Aren't you going to school anymore?"

"No. I quit."

"What are you doing now? Working?"

"No. Staying home. Loafing, I got to get a job pretty soon, though. You know how my mother is."

"Yeah," Stella said, "I sure the hell know how she is."

Eduardo took a handkerchief from his pocket and wiped the sweat beads off his brow. He was becoming increasingly nervous behind Nacho's stare. Wondering what he had done to have provoked such dislike.

Aron and Frankie came back into the room. Aron was feeling nice and heavy with pleasure behind the smack. Heavy in his easy feeling. Good feeling all over. No feeling like it in the world. Good smack running through him. Some of the best since he and Gorgey from White Fence went up on stuff. The best since then.

"You boys want a beer?" Stella asked them.

Aron shook his head. He didn't want to talk. He didn't want to say no and he didn't want to look at the beer. He wanted to sit and trip and feel good behind the feeling of horse.

"How about you," Stella said to Frankie. "Would you like a beer?"

He nodded.

She wasn't a bad looking woman. Not bad at all. Crazy to have her, he thought. Maybe later.

Eduardo, hoping to knock Nacho off his trip, said, "I like the weather we've been having. Don't you think we've been having nice weather?" The question was directed to Nacho.

Nacho didn't answer. He didn't take his eyes off Eduardo. Inside him there was a deep hate fermenting for the man he looked at.

"No smog," Stella said. "It's been good weather."

"Fucked up weather," Nacho said, looking at the man. "I don't like the weather we've been having."

"It's been okay," Sammy said, his arm around Martha.

Nacho, for the first time taking his eyes off the man, turned to Sammy. "I said it's been fucked up weather."

Sandra said, "What's the matter with you, Nacho?"

"I don't like the weather we've been having." He looked at the man and stared with a dazed hate in his eyes at the man's balding head. "I don't like you either. Whoever the fuck you are."

"Cool it," Sammy said.

"I don't like that bastard." To Eduardo, he said, "I don't like you. You hear me?"

The man could not speak. He was numb with fear.

"You're a punk," Nacho told him. "I hate punks."

"I think you better go," Stella told the man.

The man didn't move.

"You heard," Nacho said. "Split."

"What's wrong with you, Nacho," Martha said. "He ain't done nothing to you."

"I don't give a shit. I don't like the way he looks. I don't like his crooked mouth. You got a crooked mouth, you know that? I hate looking at it."

"Eduardo, please, you better leave," Stella said.

The man got up, sweat running down his face, his eyes unblinking and his pupils swelling. He reached for his coat hanging behind a chair and walked, his head bent down, out the door.

When the man left Nacho remained staring at the door the same way he had been staring at the man when he had been in the room. Nacho stared at the door a long while before he turned away from it and took a drink of his beer.

The music from the small stereo was all the noise in the room. No one was speaking. Sammy was scoring with Martha and Aron was sitting on an overstuffed arm chair, his head back, his eyes closed, listening to the music. He had paid no attention while Nacho had been hassling the man. On his face, Aron possessed a faint smile, relaxing and enjoying the smack running through his veins.

Frankie was looking at Nacho, trying to figure out what had gotten into him. He had never seen Nacho act that way toward anyone. He had remained quiet during what had been going on. He had hoped that it would end in blows between them. He was always ready to watch a good fight.

Stella was looking around, bewildered by what had occurred so abruptly. This, however, was quickly dismissed from her mind. She was now wondering about the house. She hated to clean house, unless she dropped whites. And she wasn't holding any right now. She looked around at the mess the house was in and, inwardly, she groaned.

Now, she wondered, what would happen now? There were two guys to choose from; although, looking at Aron, she was sure he was out for the night. They were young for her, she knew. However, it made no difference to her what their ages were. She had had younger dudes before. It made no difference to her whether they were old or young. They all did what guys did and it made little difference whether they were young or old. She loved the feeling either way. Sex and liquor and pills were all that made her feel. When she wasn't high or down on something she felt dead, or almost dead. Unfeeling, not loaded on something, was like being half dead. It was a bummer not to be high.

Sandra said, "What the hell got into you, Nacho?"

"I don't know," he said, reflecting. "From the first time I set eyes on him there was something about him I didn't like. It was his crooked mouth. I couldn't help myself. I just didn't like him."

Love at first sight, Sammy thought. Hate at first sight. He didn't give a fuck. He was on his trip. He had his hand cupped over Martha's breast, squeezing.

"Ouch!" Martha said. "Stop that. It hurts."

"I like to squeeze oranges in the morning," Sammy said. "There's nothing like fresh orange juice."

"Well I'm not your breakfast," she said. Then, thinking, "Or your cow."

"No, but I got a feeling I'm going to get a bedtime snack."

"Not so loud," she said.

"Let's go to the bedroom."

"No. Not now."

"Why not?"

"No."

He bit her neck and sucked it until there was a strawberry shape left when he lifted his lips away.

Nacho sat like a stone, listening to the music, remembering the man with the crooked mouth. Goddamn, how he had hated looking at it.

Sandra put her lips to his ear. She whispered, "Nacho, let's fuck."

"Where?"

"The bedroom."

"Órale."

To Stella, Sandra said, "We're going to use your bedroom."

"Help yourself," she said.

"Hold on," Sammy said. "We're going in there."

"Fuck you," Nacho said, Sandra leading him by the hand to the bedroom.

"We're coming with you," Martha said.

"Okay," said Sandra. "If you want to."

Martha and Sammy followed Nacho and Sandra to the hallway. Both couples disappeared into the bedroom and shut the door.

Frankie looked at Stella in her robe. He had a feeling she wore nothing underneath it.

"Who was that dude, anyway," he asked. "The guy that left."

"I don't know. I met him yesterday. Stayed. Spent the night, you know. Drives a bus or something."

"No, I don't like boy friends. They get, well you know, attached after a while. I like to do my own thing on my own. Know what I mean?"

"Yeah," said Frankie. "I know what you mean."

Aron opened his eyes and looked at Stella. He had had jello for dessert; his grandmother had made it especially for him. With fruit cocktail. His favorite. Sometimes he liked rice pudding. But jello with fruit cocktail was what he liked best.

He liked Stella while he looked at her. He liked the heroin in him. He thought that maybe he would like some rice pudding also.

Looking about the room, he saw an end table and he went over to it. There was a picture frame on the table. He looked at the boy in the photograph. He was in his late teens and he was dressed in a zoot-suit.

Aron rubbed the mole behind his left ear and, to Stella, said, "Who's the guy in the picture?"

"That's my brother."

"Oh yeah. Where's he at now?"

"Dead. He got killed during the riots of '43."

"I heard about them," Frankie said. "My uncle told me. He said them were some bad days."

Aron looked at the boy's face in the photograph. He somehow felt that he knew whoever it was very well.

"What was his name?"

"Everyone called him Payaso," Stella said. Then, looking more closely at Aron through drunk eyes, said, "You look a lot like him."

While rubbing the mole behind his ear, Aron studied the picture. He did look like him.

"I don't know why," he said, "but I got a feeling I know him."

"I don't see how you could," said Stella. "He's been dead for twenty-seven years."

Frankie went to sit on the couch. He said, "Stella, come over here and let's talk. Sit down."

"Wait," Aron said.

"What?" Stella said.

"Shine him on."

"Who?"

"Frankie."

"What the fuck's the matter with you?" Frankie said.

"Nothing."

"Okay then. Come here, Stella. Sit down."

"Stay where you are," Aron said.

"You nuts or something," Frankie said.

"You ain't gona lay her," Aron said.

"Who said anything about—"

"Shut up!"

"Listen, chump, I ain't asking for trouble," Frankie said. "But I ain't gonna listen to you talk to me that way."

"I ain't asking for trouble," Aron said. "You just lay off."

Frankie stood up. Pissed off. "If you're going to do anything, Aron, do it now."

From beneath his coat, Aron brought out his .38. He took it with him wherever he went.

Frankie stood staring at the gun, grinning with a flamboyant smirk.

"Put that thing away. You're acting weird, man. What's your trip?"

"You ain't gonna do shit with her, Frankie. That's all I gotta say."

"I didn't say I was going to do anything."

"Don't put on, dude. I know you."

"Sabes qué, I don't have to put up with your crazy shit." Frankie started walking toward him, slowly.

"Keep away, Frankie. I'm warning you. Keep away."

"Fuck you. You ain't got the nerve to pull the trigger. You just carry that thing around because it makes you feel like a man. You ain't no man, Aron. You're a punk. That's all you are. A stupid ass punk." Frankie kept walking.

"Stay back, Frankie."

"You ain't gonna do shit."

Aron cocked the hammer. "Move back, Frankie."

Frankie kept walking. "I wish you'd pull the trigger, punk. Because if you don't I'm going to take that gun away and ram it up your ass."

The hammer fell, dislodging lead into Frankie's heart.

In the backyard, beyond the tall wooden fence, in the alley, two dogs were copulating near some trash cans.

SOMEWHERE, SOMETIME

The gravediggers took their time. It was barely two o'clock. Jesse Mejía took a handkerchief from his hip pocket and wiped his brow. The man working next to him was Rubén Aldaña. Both of them had worked at the Evergreen Cemetery now for five years.

Jesse had seen many funerals at this cemetery. He had seen the tear-filled eyes of the bereaved, and the look of bewildered children who did not fully understand the purpose of so solemn a ceremony. Jesse whiffed at the carnation in the button hole of his jacket. Each day he picked a different flower from one of the graves. One day it would be a rose, another day it would be a carnation. In the evening when he went home, he would put the flower in a glass half filled with water. This arrangement usually had four or five flowers. When one was wilted he would throw it away. But the glass had not been empty of flowers during the five years that he had been working at the Evergreen Cemetery. Jesse looked beyond the fence of the cemetery to Brooklyn Avenue. There was another world out there. The world of the living.

He watched the cars passing on the streets and he watched the people walking on the pavements. Walking, breathing, living and every second gaining on their course toward death. Minute by minute exhausting their alloted time in the doldrums of everyday existence. *Time seeps through the fingers like a precious liquid; one tries to clutch onto it and preserve it in a futile attempt of storing it. But one tries in vain. No matter how much a person ignores this phenomenon, death conquers over us in a reminder that the irony of life ends in this mystery.*

One can only guess in earthly terms and nothing more. The bible, the so-called words of God, can be nothing more than a mere scribble, a guide book and a foundation for the basic principles of peaceful existence on earth. To say that one is going to Heaven after death is like assuming that one is going to Mars in a blimp. It's a sheer imaginative idea. Nothing more. God can surely not be the bearded messiah. The beginning and the end. There is all too much general talk going on about God. There always has been. Buddha is just as much God as Christ.

Jesse was convinced that the ultimate concept of God was beyond the reach of man. He was not religious in the formal sense. The words of the Catholic Church had never really penetrated his soul. *A man should not be a lying fool to himself. If one is going to believe, then believe without doubts.*

Jesse was a man who satisfied his higher feelings by contemplating the ideals that had plagued man since the human brain was capable of thought. His job offered him a vast amount of time to think. When he rolled around over the grass of the cemetery in the cart mower, he sometimes wandered off into deep musings. And when he was shoveling dirt into a grave he sometimes drifted into a different realm of existence, that of thinking.

Rubén Aldaña, on the other hand, did other things with his mind. Jesse glanced at him. Rubén was a man of thick skull. He was fat with a bloated face. A shade of black stubble was forever covering his face.

The element on which he feasted his brain was nothing other than a small portable radio which he carried in his shirt pocket like one carries a pack of cigarettes. This instrument of information was forever tuned in on one single station: K.F.W.B., the twenty-four hour station that filled the air with the latest death tolls, and the unending carnage that went on each day of every week to be constantly swept away by people like Jesse Mejía and Rubén Aldaña, two gravediggers that had nothing in common with each other except the same job.

At the moment Jesse was looking at Rubén with nothing less than curiosity. He and Rubén had worked together for five years. When Jesse arrived at the Evergreen Cemetery after working for the Sanitation Department for ten years, Rubén had already been here some five months. Jesse now wondered what Rubén had done with his mind before transistors came into existence. Perhaps he had been dreaming of the day when in his pocket he would carry a small box that reported to him the misfortunes of the world. Yes, Jesse thought, this must have been his dream. It was odd, too, that Rubén, though a walking receptor of world events, could not relate to you the latest bit of information with any clarity. He always told you in his own words what went through his ear, through that ear plug that was the umbilical cord to the black and silver box that slightly protruded from his pocket. He muddled everything he attempted to relate. He recited this babble without being asked. Jesse was subjugated to this relentless form of broadcasting without any desire to be listening. But he had learned not to pay any attention to Rubén. He at least had the power to shut himself off from the drab phrases that came in spurts to Rubén's lips.

Jesse Mejía was something of an intellectual, although he did not readily confess it. He considered the thoughts he pondered during his day of grave-digging nothing more than simple escapes. Just as Rubén escaped in his radio, so Jesse escaped in his mind, intellectualizing. Today he wondered, simply, why? He wondered if the ideals which man tossed around in his mind were of any importance, or something to be proud of? He had been asking himself the same questions over and over again from the days he had been collecting trash on the Eastside streets to the present as he dug graves at the Evergreen Cemetery: *What is man all about? What awaits him beyond the grave? Does one think only to pass the time, to lift oneself from the base realities of life, the savage,* oftentimes *brutal existence that was the lower realm of living, experiencing the trivialities of everyday existence? Did one think of God and other related things only to camouflage the sordidness which is the true and constant meaning of human existence?* Was getting away into a different plateau of life only a substitute for a crossword puzzle?

At the moment this was what Jesse Mejía was thinking. He thought these things while he and Rubén emptied the truck of the excess dirt that had accumulated from the graves.

Later that afternoon, Jesse and Rubén had another task before quitting for the day. There were two graves to be filled. And now they were at the first grave, shoveling in the fresh dirt onto the black box at the bottom of the six foot hole. Jesse wondered whose body lay in the coffin. Was it an old man or a young one? A woman or a girl? And what sort of chapter had that person added to the unrecorded annals of human existence? Had the person been an idiot or a genius, and what difference did it make now? Had the person been heroic or cowardly? Timid or aggressive? Beautiful or ugly?

Rubén alternated his shovelfuls of dirt with Jesse. He seemed like a robot, fulfilling his chosen duty with a state of indifference. Rubén did his task without even thinking about it. It was an automatic function with him. He was not even aware of the casket that had now disappeared under the layer of moist earth. At the moment he only knew that somewhere in the world someone had died. He knew this because the wax coated ear plug had told him just moments before that this was so.

When the grave was well covered and the earth packed tightly over the coffin, the two men began filling the rear of the truck with the excess dirt. After this was done they went on to the next grave.

At this grave they were not alone. There was a small boy by the grave. He had been there before the men arrived. He had been staring at the casket in the grave. The boy wore faded jeans and a striped T-shirt. He was barefooted and his face was smudged with streaks of dirt. Jesse recognized the familiar expression on his face, the countenance of the confused and the fearful. This look was reserved for the young. The older people had their accustomed looks at funerals or when visiting a loved one on a Sunday afternoon. All forms of expressions were held on the visitors' faces. Jesse had seen them all. The looks rarely possessed smiles. They were all looks of bereavement, of shadowy fears and uncertainties. The old faces were sometimes covered with a non-convincing appearance of understanding and a slight hint that the possessors of these faces were immortal. Only the young were honest in displaying their innocence and ignorance when in the confines of this garden of human bones and decomposing bodies. Jesse could only believe the look of the young.

The two men stood at the rear of the truck. Rubén reached for one of the shovels and said, "Last one for today, Jess."

They took their shovels and went to the mound of earth next to the grave. The boy stood at the foot of the grave, looking at the oblong box where some dirt had been cast on it by the mourners, the onlookers that had been the living satellites of the ceremony that had centered around the coffin with the pinches of dirt cast over the black stained mahogany. The dark, sad eyes of the boy were relaxed as they stared at the casket, the far away look of confusion.

Rubén adjusted the ear plug in his ear and set the tuning for better reception. Having done this, he took his shovel and pushed it into the loose earth piled over the well cut grass. He threw the earth onto the casket with the same slow motions that Jesse had seen him perform for the past five years.

The boy quickly looked away from the casket to the man who had taken his attention away from it.

"What are you doing?" he said.

"Covering the hole," said Rubén.

"But it's not even dark yet," said the boy. "The man at the gate said you didn't bury anyone until after dark."

"He's mistaken."

The next shovelful of dirt went into the grave.

"Wait," said the boy. "Don't put any more dirt into the grave."

"It's my job," said Rubén.

"Can't you wait till later? I'll be going pretty soon."

"Listen, chavalo, I've got a lot of things to do. Now why don't you just go home."

"Hold on," Jesse said. "What's the matter now?" he asked the boy. "What's so important about leaving the grave open till dark?"

"I didn't come to the funeral," he said.

"Why not?" said Jesse.

The boy looked at the grave.

"I was selling papers," he said as if apologizing to the casket. "I couldn't come. I tried. Honest. But she wouldn't let me."

Jesse said, "Who wouldn't let you?"

"My mother."

"And why not?"

"Because she never liked her." The boy looked at Jesse. "She never did like her."

"Chavalo, you're just wasting our time," said Rubén. "Run along now."

"You don't understand," said the boy.

"I understand," said Rubén. "You're wasting our time."

"We can do it later," said Jesse. "Let's go."

"Let's go!"

"Yes, let's go. We can do it later."

The two men put their shovels back in the truck then, getting aboard, they drove off. It was still day, so they agreed between themselves to go clean the windows of the caretaker.

****

The boy's eyes were glistening. He wished he could go down and wipe the dirt off the casket.

"I would have come to the funeral," he said to the grave, "but I couldn't. I wanted to come, Teresa, believe me. But my mother, you know how she is. She wouldn't let me."

Paco stared at the grave as if expecting an answer from it. He thought of the body beneath the cover of the coffin, remembering the way she looked last night at the wake. Still, serene, content. Sleeping. Nothing more. Just sleeping, he thought. Paco had stood at the rear of the chapel during the rosary. Listening quietly as he watched her family and friends at the pews. He had heard Teresa's mother crying silently all through the service. Paco had been ashamed that he had come so dirty and dressed in his paper selling clothes. Everyone else was dressed as if they were going to a fiesta. So he remained at the rear of the chapel all through the wake, self-conscious of his clothing. When it was time to pay the last respects to Teresa, Paco had been the last in line and the longest to stay and stare at Teresa's quiet face.

Now he looked at her grave and thought of today. He had quit selling his papers early today for the sole reason of going home and cleaning up so that he could go to Teresa's funeral the way she would have wished. He remembered that she had once told him that her funeral was going to be like a wedding. Lots of flowers; and people would be all dressed up and a long line of cars would parade down the streets on their way to the cemetery. Teresa always said funny things like that. And today Paco had planned on being dressed in his Sunday clothes, the ones he wore to church, to make up for last night. But his mother would not permit him and she was angered at him because he had come home too early from work. He tried to explain to her that it was Teresa's funeral, that it was necessary that he go as well dressed as possible. Then his mother said that he was going nowhere near the cemetery dressed in any form or manner. That Teresa was la hija del diablo, and that Paco had no business near her grave, to go back and finish selling his newspapers.

Instead of going back to the corner he went straight to the cemetery. Everybody was leaving and soon he was the only one standing at her grave.

The child of the devil, he thought. Why had his mother said that Teresa was the child of the devil? What he remembered of her could not be associated with any girl who might have been considered a sinner. She was not the sort of girl who teased her hair into a wild nest of strands. The sort that Paco's cousin, Jilda, was who went out with the wine drinking, dope taking lowriders of the Eastside. Teresa had been, and Paco had reserved this image only for her, saintly. Innocent. She had been a girl who had stayed mostly to herself. Paco had been one of her few friends. Teresa had been a lonely girl. Most of her time was spent in playing the piano or reading. She would sometimes read to Paco when he was over at her house. Or they would talk. He felt at ease with her and always thought of her as his older sister.

La hija del diablo? Paco could not understand why his mother had said this. He knew that she did not get along with Teresa's mother. However, this could not have been the reason for saying such a thing. True, his mother was a superstitious woman. She went around the house crossing herself every fifteen minutes. Paco could not understand this either. His mother's mind was always set in heaven. And she always used his father to allegorize this with his job, comparing God with a machinist who had control over everything that went on in the world. Paco would sometimes visualize this image with a great old man in a beard that cascaded down to his navel, thick and white with touches of gold in it. And this great old man was forever pushing buttons and pulling switches on the people of the world. A master machinist who had everything under control and who never once let events get confused to the point where he might make a mistake. He controlled everything evenly and smoothly. He had his mother cross herself regularly, and he put people behind television sets and had them stare at the luminous screen for hours at a time, and he had people doing everything that people did. He had people stop their cars long enough to buy papers from Paco, and he made people generous enough to give him tips. And this machinist did it all with his machine and his skill at the controls.

And now Teresa was in that box at the bottom of the grave. Her hands were crossed on her stomach, her face was placid and calm, and now she waited for the earth to cover her grave.

She had died three days ago at the age of twelve, coming from

confession, directly in front of the church. The story of her death was known by just about everybody on her street. It was whispered by the old women at the corner store, and talked about candidly at the kitchen table. On reflection, Paco recalled that his mother had mentioned her death as being caused by Lucifer. And, upon mentioning this, she had immediately crossed herself, looking around furtively as if Lucifer himself had overheard. And to have said this afternoon that she was the child of the devil was a statement that Paco could not understand. The moral quality of Teresa's life could not be marred by a statement like that. The fact that she been coming down the church's steps at the time of her death meant nothing. And that a dog had gone between her legs and tripped her down the steps had little relation to his mother's statement. As he had heard one woman saying last night at the wake, "I was coming out of the confessional, and when I went outside Teresa was going down the steps. Then, suddenly, this black dog went up to her and before you knew it the dog had gotten between her legs somehow and the poor girl went tumbling to her death."

From his pocket, Paco brought out a silver dollar that had been given to him as a tip. These coins were hard to come by. He looked at the coffin, at the dirt over it, and then he tossed the silver dollar over the dirt. It landed on the earth which covered the casket; the liberty head was facing the sky.

The sun was setting, disappearing behind the graveyard fence.

Looking at the coffin, Paco said, "I'll see you later, Teresa."

He walked slowly away from the grave, back to his corner to finish selling his papers.

EDDIE'S NUMBER

"Ten, twenty, thirty, forty, fifty."

Eddie counted the bills slowly into Johnny's hand.

"How long will it take you?"

"Fifteen minutes."

"You sure?"

"Yeah, yeah," Johnny said. "Fifteen minutes, no more."

The hype watched Johnny fold the five tens and slide them into his pocket. Johnny left and the hype was left waiting. He was the only one sitting inside the Donut Depot's air conditioned section. It was cool in here, and it oddly made the hype feel like he was in a glass cage. The people outside seemed to be wilting under the summer heat. Eddie watched the heat waves rise diaphanously off the asphalt of Huntington Drive. But it was cool inside the Donut Depot where the hype sat by himself. He could see shiny sweat on the people's faces outside. A little girl walked past with a Frosty Freeze cone melting in her hand. Vanilla ice cream was caked in a circle around her mouth. Her ponytail bounced behind her as she walked past the Donut Depot, not once noticing the hype that sat inside at one of the tables, silently enjoying the air conditioning around him.

The clock above his head indicated 12:30. He watched the thin red second-arm creep past the sixty notches—slowly, with all the mechanical calmness that was built into it. These moments between connections were always difficult for Eddie. There was always a sense of uncertainty behind them. But he waited as calmly as he could. He was used to waiting.

The girl behind the glass window smiled at him as she filled a cup of coke for a waiting customer outside. He liked her. He liked almost everybody when he was up on smack. He watched the girl as she walked back to the other service window with the Dixie cup in her hand. The customer paid for the coke, took the cup, and went to drink his coke in his car. The girl in the white uniform took the money from the counter and went to ring it up on the cash register.

The pleasant feeling of the fix Eddie had taken for breakfast ran through him like a soothing current. The "H" he was experiencing was some of the best horse he had had in a long time. And now, at the

Donut Depot, he wondered what sort of stuff would come his way next. Johnny told him that it was going to be nothing but the best. But they all say that. The best only comes around once in a while.

He looked at the girl again. She was sitting on a stool with her back to him. She looked like Carmen from behind. The same slim build, the same long honey colored hair. But he knew that the girl's arms were not marked by the habit, they were clean and smooth, untouched by outfit needles. Carmen worked, too. But not like the girl he looked at now. Carmen made love for her money. She made love for both their habits. No, he thought, she could never be Carmen.

The hype continued waiting for his product to arrive. The second-arm on the clock ticked on above his head. The minutes went by. One after the other. Slowly.

One is always waiting for something, he thought.

Soon the clock read 12:45. But Eddie didn't worry. They always took more time than they promised. This was one of the reasons he hated runners to score for him. There were always too many chances involved with a runner. But this time he had had no choice. His local connection was dry.

He began to feel thirsty for something sweet. The waitress was still sitting on her stool reading a movie magazine. The hype went to the counter and waited for the girl.

When she presented herself on the other side of the window, he said, "A large coke."

The waitress took a paper cup, scooped some ice in it and then she tapped the fountain for the drink.

"That'll be twenty cents."

Eddie took two dimes and put them on the counter.

"And a penny tax," said the girl.

Eddie fingered a penny from the coins in his palm and put it on the counter.

"Thank you," she said.

She rang the money up on the cash register as the hype went to sit down. He sat sipping his coke, occasionally letting a chunk of ice dissolve in his mouth.

Time passed above his head. It was now 1:30. The coke cup was now empty of coke and the hype was left sucking on the ice. He had begun to worry. The thought of having been burned was something that he kept wishing against. It was not impossible. It was the most possible thing in the world right now. But it was something he did not want to think of.

It was hot in the car. All the windows were rolled down, and warm, dry air breezed through them onto the boys that sat in the front seat.

"He ain't gonna like it," said Zeno.

"Who cares?" said Johnny.

"Eddie can get mean sometimes," said Zeno.

"I don't give a fuck if he gets mean or not. I ain't burning him. I'm just borrowing the bread to fix my car, man."

"He's going to come looking for you; and he ain't going to be too happy when he sees you."

"I'm not worried. Besides, he's got bread. He always has bread. I'll pay him back when I fix my car."

"I got a feeling he ain't gonna go for that, Johnny."

"So what? And stop worrying about it, will you?"

The hype sat at the table looking into his empty coke cup. It was 2:00. He was nervous now. He wanted to think of anything except the possibility of having been burned. Maybe Johnny ran into trouble, he thought. The cops may have come by and busted him. The hype hadn't expected to be waiting this long. He was due for another fix.

He felt the sickness coming on. It started to run through him in a merciless way, like a slimy eel circulating through his system. His blood was saturated with it. The sickness always came on slow, increasing its torture until the hype felt that he would burst with it. He had to fix again. Soon.

He looked out at the Drive, at the people walking on the hot sidewalks. He stared with glazed eyes, hoping to see Johnny coming back with the stash. The sickness was crawling over him with a devouring hunger. Sweat was breaking out over his brow. This wasn't ordinary junk sickness. The hype knew that it was something else, some disease that left a deadening effect on him whenever it came on.

He looked at the clock. He couldn't wait any longer. He had to fix. Smack would cool the sickness.

The hype went out of the Donut Depot and began walking home. The sickness held him from head to foot, swirling his mind and bringing nausea to his stomach. He walked faster, looking about to see if there were any cops around. He could not afford to get busted now. The sickness began to bring on a merciless pain that gripped his body, tearing into his nerves. He had to hold out. The sickness traveled through him with every beat of his heart. With every pound beneath his chest the thrust of the sickness entered his head like a poison and sent his stomach in a whirl. The cramps were starting and the hot and cold flashes came on. The agony that besieged him was one that he knew well. One that he had known for the last fifteen years. It was the penalty of a self-induced disease.

As the hype was coming to Eastern Avenue, he quickened his pace. His pad was just around the corner. His body now was one big bundle of paining flesh. When he saw the door of his duplex he made a dash for it; turning the knob, he pushed the door open and rushed into the house. Carmen was in the kitchen looking at herself in the mirror which she held in her hand.

"Get the stash," he said.

"Did you get the stuff?" she asked.

"Damn you! Get the stuff and start cooking!"

Carmen hopped up and began rushing around like a nurse in an emergency case. Eddie went to the bathroom for the outfit. He opened the black case and took the eye dropper out with a baby's nipple attached to it. His hands were shaking. Sweat bubbled on his brow. He readied the cap and the spoon.

"Hurry up!" he called. "Goddamn you! Carmen, hurry up!"

Carmen came rushing in with a small stamp envelope in her hand. The envelope that contained the white dust.

"Dump it!" he said. "Dump it!"

Carmen let some white powder fall into the spoon, not bothering to use the cap. She took the dropper from Eddie's shaking hand and sucked some water into it from the tap. Then, carefully, she let some drops fall into the spoon. She took the spoon from Eddie and lit a match, putting the flame under the spoon. Eddie watched the junk until it came to a boil. Carmen struck another match and waved it over the needle at the end of the eye dropper. The hype reached for it with greedy hands. The sleeve of his shirt was already pushed up and his belt was already fastened around his bicep. The vein on the arm was swollen. He tightened his fist and aimed the needle at the most recent scar on his forearm. The needle entered with a jab and the sensuousness of its penetration enraptured him down to his loins. The hype looked at the needle, pricked into his flesh. His mouth watered and saliva welled over his tongue. Eddie let the white, foggy liquid into his system, gently pressuring the nipple. The junk flowed into his blood through the tip of the needle. Not all, just a bit. A little stream of smack, nothing more. Then he drew it back in. The chamber filled with blood and mixed with the junk. He was jacking it and he was loving every plunge. The hype wanted to tease himself in his pleasure. He wanted to feel every good second of it. This time he did not want it in a quick, spasmodic jolt. This time he wanted it to ease through him like a slow come. He jacked on the nipple; into his vein and out to the chamber went the mixture of blood and junk. In and out. Then, in one heavy plunge, he let his vein take it all in.

Carmen took the spike from him and began cleaning it in the sink, letting hot water run through it. She rinsed it well and then dried it with a towel. Then she put it back in the outfit box and stashed it.

"Okay," she said. "Now, did you get it?"

The hype did not answer. He leaned against the wall enjoying the sensation of smack as it ran through his body.

"Well," said Carmen, "did you score or what?"

"Not yet."

"What do you mean not yet?"

"Just that. Not yet. I have to go back."

"What happened?"

"Johnny didn't show."

"You got burned?"

"I didn't say that. I had to come back and fix."

"You were gone a long time, Eddie."

"I know. But don't worry. You know how it goes."

"We're running low."

"Don't worry about it. I'll get it," said the hype. "How about you?"

"I got a hundred dollar trick set up on the westside. He called just after you left."

"That's good bread. Too bad you don't get more like him."

"I just might. He said he was going to introduce me to some friends of his. All money."

"You keep up like that, Carmen, and we'll be rolling in stuff."

The hype watched her as she went to the bedroom mirror. She sat and began combing her hair. Eddie looked at her with admiration as she stroked the comb through her long brown hair. He had had more than one woman in his life sharing the same life style as his. But Carmen was the prize of them all. She, though a confirmed addict of many years, still had that quality of youth and beauty. The only flaws on her body were the scars on her arms, the long acquired marks of many years of geezing. The average hype-whore like Carmen was old by thirty, used up and lame in the head, quick only to sniff out the chance of shooting dope. But not Carmen. She had class. Always neat, always clean. She never let herself go. And with or without make-up she radiated elegance and a subtle sort of innocence that gave her a girlish veneer, a poise that made her all the more desirable to the tricks that had her. And somehow, between the pattern of their relationship, he knew there was a love between them. A love that could not be defined by any definitive measure. Just one that they both knew existed. It had formed invisibly and concretely over the two years that he had known her.

The hype watched her as she arranged her curls and then held them in place with a burst of fine hair spray.

"Well," she said. "That's about it. How do I look?"

"Foxy. You look so good I feel like laying you myself."

"Tonight."

"I better get going," he said.

"Be careful."

"I'm always careful."

The hype left. Feeling good. Johnny must have scored by now, he thought. He went down the Drive more calmly now, feeling better after the fix. Yet he also felt the underlying of the sickness in him. It was a feeling of suppressed nausea that centered in the hollow of his stomach. The hype knew that this wasn't junk sickness. The junk sickness was gone and this other sickness had remained, coiled inside him as if waiting for the right moment to spring on him, like a hungry animal ready to claw up his insides.

When he arrived at the Donut Depot he asked some of the guys standing around if they had seen Johnny. They said no. He hadn't been around. For the first time Eddie felt sure that he had been burned. The thought, the realization, was upsetting. It wasn't right. Carmen worked hard for that money. She didn't get it for free. Then, it wasn't so much the money as it was the principle of the thing. The money could be got for more smack, but the idea of having someone steal it for their own purpose was what bothered him most.

He started back down the Drive, toward Eastern Avenue, to his pad. He was going for his gun. He couldn't let Johnny get away with this.

Once in the house he went to the kitchen and took his .38 out from behind the refrigerator. He opened the chamber. All six were loaded. He snapped the chamber shut and spun it. Then he put it at his waist, covering the bulge with his shirt.

As he was about to leave, the hype noticed a note on the table beside the door.

Eddie,
    I'll be back late. Don't eat all the candy.

Love,
Carmen

He put the note in his pocket and left the pad. While walking down the Drive he kept his eyes on the people, the cars, hoping to see Johnny. He wasn't going to hurt him if he didn't have to. He just wanted his money back, or the stuff. One or the other. He also watched out for squad cars. He couldn't afford to be stopped. The marks on his arms were bad enough, but these and the gun meant a sure bust, a violation of parole and a long time in jail. Time ill spent. He could do without the cages. He had too much going for him on the streets. Too much to live for; too much to stay out for. The dead weight of the gun at his waist rubbed cooly against his stomach.

The Donut Depot was on the next block. He would go there one last time, and if Johnny wasn't there he would find out where he lived and he would go looking for him there. He would find him one way or another and when he did he would take care of business.

At the corner where the Frosty Freeze was, a squad car came rounding the corner. Instead of continuing down the Drive, the squad car parked and the cop got out. Eddie stopped. He didn't think that the cop had spotted him yet. The thought struck him that he should turn around and walk the other way. But if the cop had spotted him that would only arouse his suspicion. The hype swallowed and decided to walk on and take his chances.

Eddie went toward the corner with as much cool as he could enforce. The cop was at the Frosty Freeze window placing his order. The hype went past him and was about to cross the street. Behind him now, he heard the radio calls from the squad car.

Then he heard the command. "Hey, you. Stop!"

The hype kept walking.

"I said stop!"

Eddie turned around. The cop was looking at him.

"That's right. You. Come here."

The urge to run overcame the hype. But that meant sure trouble. For a moment he was undecided as to what to do. He just stood there and stared at the cop with the ice cream cone in his hand.

"Can't you hear? I said come here!"

Eddie began walking toward him. Whatever happened, he knew he wasn't going to jail.

"I've seen you before, haven't I?" the cop said.

"I don't think so," said the hype.

"Sure I have. Highland Park. Narco. What are you up to?"

Eddie didn't answer. The cop licked his cone.

"You should clean up your ears," said the cop. "I asked you a question."

"Listen, what do you want? I haven't done anything."

"You guys are always up to something. Roll up your sleeves."

The hype didn't move. He just stood looking up into the cop's red face.

"Roll those sleeves up or you're going to the station right now."

Eddie stood his ground. They stood there, without speaking, hate in both their eyes. In a quick sweep the cop waved his hand in the air and struck the hype across the face. Then, just as quickly, the hype turned and spat at the fat red face before him. The cop dropped his cone on the walk, grabbing the hype by the shirt. He held Eddie against the car with his weight as he reached for the handcuffs. The hype squirmed beneath him and managed to take out his gun, sticking the barrel into the cop's stomach. The cop froze.

"Back off," said Eddie. "Now put your hands on the car."

Without a word, the cop obeyed. The hype unsnapped the strap on his holster and took out the gun. Then he ran around the corner to the alley. He knew that before long the neighborhood would be swarming with heat. If he could just get to the pad without being seen. He walked on, cursing Johnny and the cop under his breath. And then he felt the sickness coming on, unleashed now, running wild in his blood. His stomach heaved and he stopped a moment to vomit. The miasma of the sickness spun his head, weakening him. He walked on, the smell of vomit on his breath. His heart pounding beneath his shirt.

When he came to the street he looked around before crossing to the next alley. He began to run. His vision blurred and his legs felt like rubber bands. He turned onto the next alley that joined with the one he was on. Then his legs folded beneath him and he stumbled and fell. He sat there resting against the door of a garage. Everything was spinning around him. His stomach heaved and he puked up air, gagging on his saliva. He attempted to get up but he found this difficult to do.

Then he saw the black & white car before him in a blur.

"I've got you covered," the cop said, behind the car with a shotgun. "Throw the guns out."

The hype rubbed his eyes with his hand to clear them. He lifted the gun with an effort and cocked it, firing one shot. Then another and another.

From behind the squad car, the cop pulled the trigger, scattering the hype on the ground.

Shortly after this, people began to gather around the scene. They stared at the hype's still body with curiosity. More squad cars came and the cop who shot him said that the hype was dead.

But while the news cameras reeled off their film, recording the scene for the six o'clock news, the hype opened his eyes. He could see the blood that was dripping from his nose and he felt the sickness emptying from him. He heard the people around him, talking and whispering and wondering what had happened. And in his mind the hype saw a beach of pearl white sand, long and curving into a bulbous peninsula. There was nobody on the beach. And over the sound large gulls with lengthy needle-like bills were flying the cloudless sky. They were floating on the air currents and diving from their high flights into the sea below. Then, with a roar the sea cast a rolling wave onto the beach and when it broke, a boy, naked and bronzed by the sun, came walking onto the white sand.

The hype smiled and closed his eyes.

SCATTERBRAIN JOHNNY

David had his .22 revolver and rifle that night. They were riding in Denny's car, smoking weed and drinking beer. It was the first time David had met Johnny. From the very start David had pinned him down as a scatter brain character. They had gone cruising on Monterey Road, putting out street lamps as they fired shells out the window. They could think of nothing else to shoot at without having the law fast on their trail. Street lamps were the only safe targets they could find. Johnny was getting his nut from shooting at the lights.

He would say, "Let me do it again. Come on guys. One more time, please. Just one last time." And David would laugh and hand Johnny the revolver and on would come this clown-like smile on Johnny's mug, his eyes bulged behind his glasses and his hand feeling the coolness of the gun. Everytime he would put out a street lamp he would laugh until he began to cough up oysters and spit them out the window. Then he would wipe his mouth with a gummy looking rag he carried in his back pocket and he would aim the gun at another yellow light that hung from the wires that passed above the car.

Leaving a considerable amount of darkness behind them, after a while, they got bored shooting at street lamps. Except for Johnny. He could have shot every light out in the neighborhood without ever thinking twice about the cops.

Denny drove the car into El Sereno, taking the back streets to avoid the law. They ended up behind the El Sereno Playground in Hillside Village. He parked the car on a dead-end street at the bottom of the hill and they got out. Then they walked up the slope of a hill. It must have been two in the morning.

When they reached the top of the hill, they saw that the earth was barren and thin, sick weeds were scattered here and there among rocks. It was still and quiet on the hill. Below them was an El Sereno neighborhood. The next day must have been trash day because the curving streets were lined with trash cans and boxes. The early morning was serene, indeed, as if the night had geezed before coming on. The street lamps were dimmed by light fog and the lamps themselves were ornamented with glowing auras.

"Let's shoot at those pads down there," said David, and then waited to hear what the others thought.

"I don't care," said Johnny. "It's up to you guys." He adjusted his glasses and then thrust his hands into his black trench coat. The coat was two sizes too large for him. It fit him loose and came down to his ankles.

Denny had the rifle and David had the revolver.

"How about the parked car down there," said Johnny. "The red one. Or the trash can next to it."

"No," said David. "No. Something big. We need something big to shoot at."

"Shoot into one of the windows," Denny said.

"You take the first shot."

"*You* take the first shot."

"You've got the rifle," said David.

"I'll trade."

"Wait," said David. "I know what we can shoot at."

"What?"

David turned to Johnny who was kicking some stones with his foot.

David stepped toward Johnny with this new thing in his head and said, "Let's shoot him."

Johnny raised his eyes to meet David's stare, gun in hand, smiling into Johnny's mug.

In a sudden realization of what was happening, Johnny flinched convulsively and tensed his body.

David began circling Johnny, walking slowly around him, not taking his eyes off him, smiling wide. The gun. The bullet in the chamber peeking down the barrel to Johnny's gut. And then, attuned to the trip, Denny began circling. They circled and held Johnny in the center.

Johnny, lifting the collar of his trench coat up to the back of his head, said, "Come on, you guys, don't. Cut it out. Come on."

Johnny's feet began to jitter and shuffle.

"We're going to blast your head off, Scatter Brain Johnny," David said. "How do you like *that*?" His arm stretched, aiming for Johnny between the eyes. "We're going to make a *real* scatter brain out of you," and then he chuckled behind his crazy grin.

"Denny, tell him I'm okay. Tell him to leave me alone, Denny."

Denny, though, wasn't about to say anything. He found himself grinning right along with David as he lifted the rifle to take aim, catching Johnny's head dead-center, walking slowly around him. There was a light, tingling, pleasurable feeling in the finger that pressured the trigger. It would be easy to pull it back, he thought. So very easy.

Johnny was twisting himself into all kinds of postures, pulling his coat over his head as if that would prevent the bullet from shattering his skull.

"Cut it out, you guys. Come on. Leave me alone. *Stop!*" He jumped around in a frenzy. Jumping and hopping, not knowing what to do with himself.

David said, "On the count of three, Denny, pull the trigger." And then, slowly, he began to count off the numbers. ". . . One . . . Two . . . Okay. Get ready."

"*DON'T! PLEASE DON'T KILL ME!*"

"THREE!"

"BOOM!"

"BOOM!"

"BOOM!"

"BOOM!"

When Johnny opened his eyes, David went up to him and patted him on the back. "You're okay, Johnny. We wouldn't do anything to you." He sounded like a counselor in Juvy Hall reassuring a trembling kid.

They went back to the car after that. Denny and David were laughing among themselves. Johnny only grinned and kept quiet.

IN THE PARK

SCENE: A park bench. LAURA is sitting at one end of the bench. The WINO is standing behind the center of the bench. There is the SOUND of a MERRY-GO-ROUND in BACKGROUND. Laura is shelling and eating peanuts from a bag. STEVE ENTERS, stage left. He is very casual as he comes in. Laura and Steve look at each other. They are not aware that the wino is there all through the scene. Shortly after Steve comes in, he sits at the opposite end from Laura. He looks at her and then out at the park; she looks at him, turns away; he looks at her, turns away, etc. This goes on for a while of nervous anticipation. The wino during this time is watching them as if watching a ping pong game.

STEVE
Sure is a nice day, isn't it?

WINO
(taking in a deep breath)
Sure is.

LAURA
Were you speaking to me?

STEVE
Who else would I be speaking to?

WINO
Me.

LAURA
Yes . . . I guess it is a nice day.

STEVE
(after pause)
Do you come here often?

WINO
Often enough.

LAURA

Where?

STEVE

Here. To the park.

LAURA

Yes. I usually come here on Sundays with my father. He sells peanuts here.

STEVE

Really? Is he the one that goes around pushing a white cart, yelling, "Cacahuates calientes!"?

LAURA
(slight laughter)

Yes. That's him.

STEVE

I see him practically everytime I come here.

LAURA

Do you come here a lot, too?

STEVE

Mostly on Sundays, like you. I like to come here and meditate, walk around and things like that.

LAURA

That's when my father comes here. On Saturdays and Sundays. You see, it's only a hobby with him. Selling peanuts, I mean. He's a garbage collector on weekdays.

STEVE

That's a strange hobby. A garbage collector who sells peanuts on weekends. He must be quite a guy.

LAURA

He is. He's really a very nice man. Even though some people think he's crazy.

STEVE

Why should they think he's crazy?

LAURA

You know how people are. If you like to do something that's not done ordinarily, they think you're crazy. My father doesn't sell peanuts because he has to. He sells peanuts because he likes to. It's no different than collecting stamps.

STEVE

I don't think selling peanuts on weekends is crazy. My grandfather used to sell tamales on First Street. It wasn't just a hobby with him. He sold tamales everyday of the week. Near the cemetery. He wasn't crazy. He was just a very independent person. Some people are like that. They either can't stand working for people, or they can't stand people. So they become independent merchants, or winos or hermits, or some anti-social person like that. My grandfather never liked working for anyone. He used to tell me, "When I work for someone else I may make more money, but I'm not as happy as I am when I work for myself."

WINO

That must have been old Tomás. A regular crook, that one. Sometimes when he didn't have beef or pork he would sell dog food in those things he called food. A regular crook. I knew him well.

STEVE

He's dead now. My grandfather.

WINO

That's a matter of opinion. It's such a confusing word.

STEVE

Died of a heart attack one day while selling his tamales. My mother used to tell him, "You're pushing that cart too much. You should take a vacation." But no. He was up every morning at three making his tamales, and he would work all day long until twelve at night.

WINO

I still see him sometimes when I'm down on First. He's usually standing there on the corner where he keeled over, standing and looking at the people he used to sell his ta-

males to. For some reason I don't think he can get over the
fact that he's dead.

STEVE

He was a kindhearted old man. His name was Tomás.
"Tomás de los tamales," that's what they knew him by.

LAURA

My father probably knew him. He used to sell peanuts
down on First. He still does. But not as often as he used
to. I guess he sort of likes Lincoln Park. He knows practically everybody that comes here. Sometimes, when he's
invited, he quits early and joins someone's picnic and
drinks beer for the rest of the afternoon, talking and playing cards, you know. (looks at bag of peanuts) Oh, I'm
sorry. Would you care for some peanuts?

STEVE
(reaching in bag)

Thanks.

LAURA

By the way, my name's Laura.

STEVE

Glad to meet you, Laura. My name's Steve.

WINO

And my name's Bruce. Could you spare a quarter for a
bowl of soup?

LAURA

Do you live around here?

WINO

No one pays attention to you when you're dead.

STEVE

Nearby. A few blocks away. You know where that new
hot dog stand is on Main?

LAURA

Yeah.

STEVE
Well, besides working there, I live right around the corner from it. And you?

LAURA
I live in El Sereno. By the playground.

STEVE
By the El Sereno Playground?

LAURA
Yeah.

STEVE
(surprised)
Really!

LAURA
Really.

STEVE
Say, I'm usually down there on Saturday afternoons. I go down there to play basketball. Do you go to the playground often?

LAURA
Not lately. I usually work on Saturdays.

STEVE
Oh . . . What do you do? I mean, where do you work?

LAURA
Nowhere in particular. I'm a dancer. A topless dancer.

STEVE
(dumbfounded)
You . . . you're a topless . . . dancer?

LAURA
Yes. Does it surprise you?

WINO
It shouldn't. She has a lot of talent. More than most. She

can really move. I suppose that's why I always considered
her my favorite niece.

> STEVE
> (recovering)
> No, it doesn't surprise me. It's just . . . well, I would have
> never taken you for a topless dancer. That is, I've never
> met a topless dancer.

> LAURA
> It's not unusual to be a topless dancer nowadays. I'm not
> making a career out of it, you understand. I'm just doing it
> to get me through college. The job pays well. And I really
> have no gripes about exposing myself. Dancing is one of
> the most natural things in the world. And as far as being
> nude, well how natural can one get?

> STEVE
> (swallows)
> Where do you work? Maybe I'll come down and see you
> dance sometime.

> LAURA
> Everywhere. We never work in any one place twice in a
> row. The agency keeps moving us around. For our own
> protection, if you know what I mean. They got some real
> kooks that go into those places. Anyway, I won't know
> about my week's assignments until tomorrow morning.

> STEVE
> (disappointed)
> Oh.

> LAURA
> But if you really want to come down and see me dance. I
> could give you my phone number and you could call me.
> I'll let you know where I'll be as soon as I find out.

> STEVE
> Hey, that's great.

(Steve reaches in his back pocket for paper and in his shirt pocket for
pen. Wino here repeats the number in sequence with Laura.)

LAURA

228-4962.

STEVE

What was that again?

LAURA (and WINO)

228-4962.

STEVE
(putting paper and pen away)
What time will you know where you'll be dancing?

LAURA

I should know by noon. This is an evening week for me.
Which means I'll be working evening. Last week I worked
afternoons.

STEVE

It must be interesting work.

LAURA

It is. Believe me.

STEVE

How long have you been doing that sort of work?

LAURA

Oh, about six months now. It's not too bad after you get
used to it.

WINO

Nothing is too bad after you get used to it. It even takes
time to get used to being dead. It even takes time to being
dead even if you're alive.

STEVE

Do you ever run into trouble doing what you do?

LAURA

Not really. Oh, I get pinched here and there. But that's
about it. Nothing serious. . . . But wait, I just remembered:
You're not going to believe this, but I swear to God, I saw
this old man one night on his knees, I swear to God, *kneel-*

ing! saying the rosary! (cracks up) I swear! He was on his knees praying, looking up at me while I was dancing. And I could see sweat running down his wrinkled face in the dim light. Sweat was all over his face like if he was running a high fever or something, and I could see his lips moving silently while he fingered the beads. It was too much, let me tell you. I never saw anything like that before in my life. And nobody was doing anything about it. I mean everyone was looking at him as if it were normal for him to be there praying on his knees. I guess he used to do that every night, because nobody paid attention to him. Smoke was curling everywhere around him, the juke box was wailing, and the billiard balls were clicking in the background, and this old man was on his knees saying the rosary, staring at me while I danced. He never smiled or took his eyes off me once, not even when I sat down. All through the evening he knelt on the floor with the same glass of milk in front of him on the table. It was a strange experience for me. I mean I'm used to being stared at when I'm up there dancing, practically nude with all those eyes on me. But I've never seen anything like that old man before. And I've never felt like he made me feel either. Honest, he made me feel like a saint, an unholy, evil kind of saint.

STEVE
Maybe he was so drunk he thought he was in church.

LAURA
That's just it. He *was* in church. I mean, in his own far out mind, in his own sick reality he was very much in church.

STEVE
Well, it takes all kinds.

LAURA
It sure does. But you know what was so weird, Steve?

STEVE
What?

LAURA
The old man looked like a Jew. I swear.

STEVE
What's so strange about that?

LAURA

The rosary. How many Jews say the rosary?

STEVE

As far as that goes, how many people say the rosary in a
topless joint? The old man was obviously a nut.

WINO

To say the least.

LAURA

I suppose it makes no difference what he was. Like you
said, it takes all kinds.

STEVE

Didn't you say you were going to college?

LAURA

Not now. I will be going next quarter, though. Right now
I'm saving as much money as I can. I don't want to have to
work when I go to school.

STEVE

What will you be taking up?

LAURA

Parapsychology.

STEVE

Para-what?

LAURA

Parapsychology. The study of the supernatural. E.S.P.,
telepathy, ghosts. Things like that.

STEVE

Ghosts?

LAURA

Sure. Don't you believe in ghosts?

STEVE

No. Not really. I have no reason to.

WINO

This kid has a lot to learn.

LAURA

I didn't believe in ghosts either. Until I saw one.

STEVE

You saw a ghost?

LAURA

Not only did I see a ghost, but my father saw one as well.
The same one in fact.

WINO

Sure did.

LAURA

It was my Uncle Bruce. My father's brother. He died on
this very bench. Right here (pats bench) on this very
bench. They found him one morning still as a rail, laying
down with an empty bottle of wine clasped in his hands.

WINO
(directly to Steve)
You'd die too if you sat there drinking wine for three
days. The early morning gets very cold around here.

LAURA

My father saw him one Sunday afternoon while he was
pushing his cart by here. My uncle was sitting here reading
a newspaper. My father couldn't believe his eyes at first. I
mean, you can just imagine what he felt like. Seeing his
dead brother on this bench reading a newspaper. My father
just stood there staring at him; and then my uncle said,
"Good afternoon, Mateo. Can you spare a dime for a cup
of coffee?" I guess my uncle was just being funny. Can
you imagine a dead man drinking coffee?. . . Anyway, my
father was struck dumb. Finally, he asked my uncle what
he was doing there. He said, "You're supposed to be dead,
Bruce." My uncle said, "I am dead." And my father said,
"Well then what are you doing there reading the paper?"
And my uncle said, "Just sitting. There's hardly anything
to do when you're dead." So they both sat here on this
very bench and had a long conversation on what it's like to

be dead. I know it sounds unbelievable. I didn't believe it
myself to tell you the truth. Neither did the rest of my
family. My mother accused my father of being drunk. But
my father doesn't get drunk. He drinks, but he never gets
drunk. And he's just as sane as you or me. Like I said, I
didn't believe it myself—at first. Then, a few weeks later,
while I was dancing at the Purple Eye in El Monte, in
comes my Uncle Bruce. I stopped dancing dead in my
tracks and just stared at him. All the men in the place were
getting angry because I wasn't dancing. They were saying,
"Move it, baby. Move it." You know how they get. But I
couldn't move for the life of me. I couldn't do anything
but just stare at my uncle. He was standing by the bar
smiling at me, and then he waved at me. After that he just
disappeared. Vanished. Like in the movies, I swear, he just
vanished into thin air.

                          STEVE
That's some story. But maybe you were just seeing things.

                          LAURA
That's what I kept telling myself. But I couldn't convince
myself of that. If it would have been just me that saw my
Uncle Bruce, then maybe I would have let it go at that.
But my father saw him too, and talked to him to boot.
And if nobody else believes him, I do, because I saw the
very same thing.

                          STEVE
Well, there's no way for me to disprove it.

                          LAURA
And there's no way to prove it either. But there's one
thing I can say. There's a lot more to living and dying than
one may think. (Wino nods his head in agreement) Most
people don't believe anything in this so-called natural
world unless it's concrete. But there's a lot more dimensions in this world than we can count. I know it sounds
abstract, but— . . . Well, let's leave it at that. . . . Anyway,
how do we know that my uncle isn't standing right next to
us this very minute?

                          STEVE
                     (looking around)
We don't . . . I guess.

WINO

She's a bright little cookie. A good dancer, too. If I were alive I would have taken her for a nut, though. After all, how many people believe in ghosts?

STEVE

Have you got any more peanuts?

LAURA
(looking in bag)
No. (looks out at park) But there's my father over there. Let's go get some more.

STEVE

Okay.

(They exit stage right. Wino stretches and yawns and walks around to the bench. From his back pocket he takes out an empty wine bottle, and then he lays down on the bench and puts the bottle on his chest, clasped in his hands.)

CURTAIN

BLUE DAY ON MAIN STREET

EDITORS: QUINTO SOL PUBLICATIONS

HERMINIO RIOS-C.   OCTAVIO I. ROMANO-V.